Twins Alex and Zeca love to switch identities. It's harmless fun until Alex wants to date a hot tourist visiting their home of Capri and asks Zeca to take his place on a date with Alex's current beau, Antonio.

After a day in Antonio's arms—followed by a long, lusty weekend in his bed during a trip to Naples—Zeca discovers switching places with Alex isn't so harmless after all. Especially when he realizes he's falling hard for his brother's boyfriend.

While struggling with his feelings for Antonio, consoling his semi-celebrity father (who's having woman troubles) and trying not to upset Alex (who might be in love with Antonio...or his tourist tryst...or maybe the neighbor lady), Zeca wonders how any of them will make it through all the relationship woes with hearts intact. As Antonio says, "Love has a way of fixing things itself."

This book has been previously published.

Relentless Passion
Copyright © 2019 A.J. Llewellyn
ISBN: 978-1-4874-2494-7
Cover art by Martine Jardin

Published by eXtasy Books Inc or
Devine Destinies, an imprint of eXtasy Books Inc

Look for us online at:
www.eXtasybooks.com or www.devinedestinies.com

Relentless Passion
Relentless Book 1

By

A.J. Llewellyn

DEDICATION

To my readers with love!

Trademarks Acknowledgement

The author acknowledges the trademarked status and trademark owners of the following wordmarks mentioned in this work of fiction:

Band-Aid: Johnson & Johnson Corporation
Clairol: The Procter & Gamble Company
Evian: Societe Anonyme Des Eaux Minérales D'Evian
Fiat: Fiat S.P.A. Italy
I Love Lucy: CBS Broadcasting Inc.
iPod: Apple Inc.
Levi's: Levi Strauss & Co.
London Stock Exchange: London Stock Exchange Limited LC
Luigi Borrelli: Aluc Mark Anstalt Corporation
Smithsonian: Smithsonian Institution Trust Instrumentality
Timberland: The Timberland Company
Triumph: Bayerische Motoren Werke AG
TV Times: Athlon Sports Communications, Inc. dba Athlon Media Group Corporation
Vogue Italia: Advance Magazine Publishers Inc.

CHAPTER ONE

"So, what do you think?"

"What do I think about . . . what?"

It was hard to tear my gaze away from the handsome man walking away from the break table outside our father's restaurant. The sun shone, and I could hear imaginary violins in the air as my eyes made love to the sexy man with the perfect ass. His white jeans showed off his masculine attributes as he strolled along the terraced piazza. Aware of our gazes, he turned and winked.

I almost swallowed my spoon.

"Dang," my brother Alex said.

I heard my father cursing as the coffee grinder fritzed again. "Zeca!"

Yep, I was Dad's go-to guy. Pity he wouldn't be mine. I wanted to try out his incredible, new — to him — snow-white 1960 Triumph Herald coupe. It was only one of one hundred and sixty-two left in the world, but he said I was reckless. That galled me, considering my twin, Alex, was a far worse driver than me.

"But he's older than you, more reliable," my dad loved to say. Yeah, older by two whole minutes.

I got up from my seat, imagining myself with the hottie in the white jeans, driving around Capri, the sun in our faces, the wind in our hair . . .

And the coffee grinder, for all intents and purposes, dead on arrival.

"Congratulations," I told my father.

He beamed. "You fixed it!"

"No, Dad. You killed it."

"Why the congratulations, then?"

"You have no more excuses. You can finally donate it to the Smithsonian."

My father's eyes narrowed. "It's not that old."

"Yes, it is. Face it. It had a long life, never met a cup of coffee it didn't like. Let's give it a decent burial."

"What, you don't even think it's a museum piece now?"

I unplugged the unit, which had made more comebacks from the grave than your average atomic-fueled zombie, and swept up all the coffee grounds with the little wicker broom we kept for the countertops. I emptied the coffee into the container of grounds that would later be used on our plants.

My father's pride and joy, apart from his coffee, was his green thumb. Short of chopping it off and selling it, he marketed Toppy's Homemade Fertilizer. Tourists bought it by the bag, partly because of my dad's semi-celebrity status. Toppy Colombo had played a café owner in a British TV soap opera for twenty-five years. He was a handsome man, still in damn fine shape. His dark hair had no gray in it, thanks to a close relationship with infinite bottles of Clairol's Natural Black. He also had sparkling white teeth. Since he considered them one his most valuable assets, he made sure they showed each time he smiled, when he wasn't bullshitting the ladies with his flirting.

The locals rolled their eyes. They felt Toppy could have marketed his brand of BS along with everything else we stocked on our shelves.

Like everybody else on Via Camerelle, the main shopping strip on Capri, we sold a lot of lemon products. The whole island was geared toward the manufacture of anything to do with lemons. And lots of designer boutiques had luxurious addresses on Via Camerelle, but for my dad, his dream of a restaurant had come true. He was a big success. The guide-books all listed his café as a highlight of Via Camerelle. Sandwiched between a gourmet chocolate shop and a shoe store, the café got a lot of cross traffic. Hence, we never stopped moving behind the counter at Café Toppy.

Alex followed me to the back room, where I dumped the grinder into a box to toss out later. I hunted out a good hiding spot, knowing the second my dad got some extra time he'd repair the thing with super glue, rubber bands, chewing gum ... you name it. Alex and I had bought a new industrial-strength grinder, and I removed it from its hiding place, ripping open the elaborate packaging Italian coffee companies seem to love so well.

"So ... will you do it for me?"

"Do what?" I asked, exasperated.

He slapped his head, one of the least attractive traits he'd picked up from Dad. "Will you go out with Antonio for me tonight?"

I stared at him. Is that what he'd been blathering on about outside? I'd been so busy bulge and ass watching I hadn't heard a word Alex had said.

Antonio was a good-looking guy. Damn good-looking, in fact. Alex and I had always loved pulling pranks on prospective dates by switching identities. It was usually harmless fun since nobody could tell us apart, even our dad, for that matter, but Antonio was a hot mofo.

"You sure?" I asked him. "He's ..."

"Gorgeous. Yeah, I know." Alex grinned. "Truth is, I've met an even hotter guy."

"Who? Where?"

He gazed at me, and I wanted to scream. "Not the cutie in the white jeans?"

He lifted his shoulders. "Yeah. Sorry."

"How? When?"

"He slipped me his number while you were busy licking foam off your cappuccino cup. You know, you really oughta get a life. You licked that cup clean."

"I know, I'm pathetic. How bad is Antonio if you want *me* to date him?"

"You're not pathetic. Neither is he. I don't want to blow him off. He's nice . . . I'm just . . ."

"Greedy?"

"Lucky," he insisted. This was true. "Listen, it's just one date. Hugh's only in town a couple more days. I really want to see him . . . please?"

"Hugh." I swallowed. "You know his name."

"Of course I know his name. He hit on me. I can hardly call him 'hey, you' all night."

"I don't know." I liked Antonio. He certainly seemed smitten with my brother, and that was the problem. He liked my twin, not me. And that was common. Guys always went for Alex before me because, for all our physical similarities, his personality was amazing. Mine wasn't. I was shy; so shy that, by the time I worked up the courage to hit on a guy, he was three time zones away getting married to some other man.

Alex and I were blessed with Dad's dark hair, his appealing looks, brown eyes, vibrant health, and all our own teeth. In fact, we took pride in being the exception to all the jokes about the British and their teeth. And I guess since Alex zoomed out of our mother's womb first, he snatched up all the charisma.

"No," I said.

"Why not?"

Antonio was handsome, sexy, fun, smart, and, I thought, probably successful and charming. All the things Alex and I liked in a guy. They hadn't dated enough that Antonio could really tell us apart, but still, there was something about the guy that made me wary of trying to pull a fast one on him.

"Well . . . he's smart," I said. "He'll know I'm not you."

"A little limoncello in you, buddy, and you'll be so re-laxed, just like me. Just smile a lot and laugh at his jokes."

"You make this sound like a pity date."

"It's not. Well . . . *he's* not in need of my pity. You are. When was the last time you had some action?"

Too long. "Are you sure?"

"Sure I'm sure."

Something still didn't sit right with me. "Okay, what's wrong with him?"

"Nothing *wrong* with him." Alex shrugged again. "The new guy is hotter."

"How far have you gone with Antonio?"

"Nothing, just kisses. It's only been three dates."

"And what does he do for a living?"

"He owns a restaurant in Naples."

"Oh, okay."

Naples was one of the three closest cities people came from every weekend, storming the island of Capri in search of unspoiled, relaxed magnificence. If he was in the restau-rant business, we could talk shop. That would give us some common ground. I wondered if he, like me, ever had recur-ring nightmares of running out of teaspoons.

Alex clasped my arm. "He's getting the ferry across from Naples this afternoon. I'm supposed to meet him at the fu-nicular when it comes up to the village."

"No . . . I don't think so. This guy's going to a lot of trou-ble to see you. I think you're being kind of tacky, Alex."

"Dad's letting me drive the Triumph tonight. If you do this, I'll let you drive it instead."

I blinked. "Give me the keys. Now."

Sunday afternoons in Capri are my favorite times in the world. Everyone is having a siesta. Even the island dogs stop barking. Everything is closed for at least three hours. The sun is warm, not too hot, most of the year. You can smell lemons growing even in tiny containers on many people's balconies. Without fail, somebody will pop their head out of their store or house and offer me a taste of the local liqueur, homemade limoncello, a lemon peel cookie or, if I'm really lucky, a sliver of lemon tart. I always accept. Just to be polite, you know. It's a useful way to numb myself as I climb the eighty-eight limestone steps from the piazza to our street, which is nestled high in the hills.

That's the thing about Capri. You just keep climbing. More stairs? Another long and winding road? *Here, have a drink.*

Our nearest neighbor bakes succulent combinations of lemon, olive, and rosemary bread on Sundays and you can smell the results up and down the entire street whilst you nap. My father always says you can tell when it's time to wake up when you no longer smell the bread baking. But then, my father's keen sense of smell has a lot to do with the fact that he's bedding the baker, the recently widowed Angelina Langoni. It's one of the worst-kept secrets on the island.

His Capri Town home is right next door to hers. Their siestas and nighttime frolics are conducted in private in her home, but he isn't fooling anyone, sneaking in and out of our house via the back door morning, noon, and night.

Divorced from our mother for twelve years, our retired actor father had pined for love after a series of romantic disasters. He moved to his childhood home of Capri and bought the restaurant after the owner decided to move back to Rome. Toppy then snapped up a gorgeous cliff-side house and the hormonally bereft Angelina Langoni. She was a beautiful woman by anyone's standards. Dad prided himself on snagging her fast. He also got the best bread on the island out of the deal.

Coaxing Alex and me to Capri from our dreary stock-broker jobs in London had been a rare stroke of genius on Toppy's part. Having me and Alex in the house meant that we, the local gay twins, gave the islanders fresh fodder. Nobody knew what was going on in our house and we didn't care what crazy stories they made up about us. Sad thing was, the gossip was so much more interesting than the truth.

At the age of twenty-eight, I was enjoying my sixth month on the island, even if I hadn't had much action. I worked hard and looked forward to my daily naps, particularly on Sunday, because Angelina, as a favor to us, started baking cinnamon bread on Sundays. The scent was intoxicating, and I always woke excited, knowing the bread was just for us.

I was in the middle of a really, really good nap, my mind on white jeans and cute butts and, God help me, floating images of broken coffee grinders. Well, maybe just one coffee grinder, but it was a persistent, ominous-looking one. I was awakened by a loud thumping on our front door. My room was on the top floor of the house, a narrow terrace above the equally narrow cliff road. My dad's room was opposite mine, and Alex's was down the hall next to his. I poked my head out the window and saw Antonio on the street below me.

He looked handsome in his jeans and black silk shirt as he gazed up and waved. "Hey, beautiful."

I stifled a yawn. "Um . . . hey yourself. Did the ferry get in already?"

"Ferry?"

"You were coming by ferry from Naples, right?"

"Naples? No, *tesoro*." He wrinkled his nose up at me, his expression perplexed. "Why did you think I was in Naples?"

Oh my God.

"I'll let you in."

I ran to Alex's room, but the bastard wasn't there. I was going to get him for this. Rule number one when you plan on switching identities—get your facts straight. I went downstairs and threw open the door.

Antonio stood there, grinning. "Wow . . . this is a fantasy come true."

He thought I was a fantasy? Man! With his dark hair, classic Italian looks, piercing blue eyes, and kissable mouth, he was the hottest man I'd ever seen. He stepped inside and slid his arms around me.

Holy shit! I forgot I'm just wearing underpants!

His hands roamed my ass, which was encased in tight, white boxer briefs, and I felt myself responding in a way that was completely inappropriate considering he was my brother's boyfriend.

Damn that Alex. Antonio was *hot*. I'd met him twice like I said, but I'd forgotten how sexy he was. The man radiated an erotic aura that was dangerous when I hadn't had a date in months, and my dreams were haunted by angry coffee grinders.

He kissed me.

I didn't resist. *This is what Alex would do.*

Hell, Antonio was the hottest thing I'd seen on two legs in a long time, even if he wasn't wearing white jeans. I felt the bulge in his jeans harden against me.

Oh man. Not good. I broke off the kiss, stepping back from him.

He stared at me, his gaze moving from my lips to my obvious erection. He wagged a finger. "That was the best kiss you ever gave me. You . . . you're on fire, I think."

Yeah. I'm a regular disco inferno. The kiss was so electrifying I wanted to do it again. And again. I mentally bitch-slapped myself.

"Oh. Um. Thanks." I backed away farther. "Take a seat,

I'll go get dressed."

"What a pity." His mouth quirked into a smile. "Don't forget your swimsuit."

Swimsuit? Up in my room, I called my brother, pacing as I tried to find some swim trunks that didn't scream *fuck me!*

"Hey," he said, picking up on the ten-thousandth ring.

"Listen," I hissed. "You told me he was coming from Naples by ferry. Wrong."

"Oh, really? I'm sure he mentioned the ferry."

"And he said I need a swimsuit. What kind of date am I going on?"

"Oh. Swimming and dinner."

"Well, I can do that. Now listen, are you *sure* he owns a restaurant?"

I could hear laughter in the background.

"Where are you?" I asked.

"Next door with Dad and Angelina. She just baked cinnamon bread."

I was about to say something rude when he reminded me I had a date waiting downstairs.

"Don't eat all the bread. Bring some home," I said, but he'd already ended the call. I found some swim trunks and slipped them on. Black and white. Small, but not obscene. My cell phone rang. It was Alex, talking with his mouth full.

"He bought me a blue shirt. It's in a bag in my room. Make sure you wear it, he keeps asking me about it."

Once again he ended the call, and I ran to his room. Out his side window, I caught a glimpse of our other neighbor, Mrs. Pampina, doing nude aerobics. I'd never realized Alex could see right into her bedroom.

I'd also never seen such massive tits before. Or anyone so, er . . . over-generously proportioned.

My eyes! My eyes! I tried to cover them, tried not to look. It was a car wreck in motion. She caught my gaze and suddenly, her husband reached across the window and slammed their shutters closed.

Oh great. Next rumor running around Capri would be that I coveted my neighbor's wife.

No, wait. This was Alex's room. My day was looking up. He might have gotten the guy in the white jeans, but he now had an irate Italian husband on his hands as well.

I turned my attention to finding the blue shirt. My brother had a plethora of beaus who had constant urges to gift him with beautiful things. *I* got the broken coffeemakers to sort out. I found three shopping bags, one of which contained a blue, pin-striped Luigi Borrelli shirt. It was about the most exquisite thing I'd ever seen . . . without legs, that is.

Borrelli was the most luxurious, highly prized shirtmaker. Wow, Antonio really liked my brother.

I slipped the shirt on, let it hang over my vintage button-down Levi's and felt sexy. Damn. I looked like all the other Italian hipsters. A new look for me. My normal couture was jeans, running shoes, and a perpetual look of anxiety. I started to feel like Alex. I stood in his room and breathed deeply, channeling my inner charm school graduate. I took one more look at the shirt. It was a little formal, but it was a wonderful piece of fabric. Even without benefit of a cocktail, I felt pretty good.

Walking downstairs with my Timberland loafers in my hand, I saw Antonio's expectant smile fading into a frown as he gazed up at me from the sofa.

"Isn't that a little dressy? Why don't you wear the shirt I gave you?"

My Alex smile froze on my Zeca face, and I ran back upstairs.

Where the hell was his blue shirt?

I ransacked Alex's room for a bag containing another blue shirt and couldn't find one. I called my brother.

"Are you still there?" he asked in an agonized tone.

"Where the hell is the blue shirt? I put on the Borrelli, and it's not the one he gave you."

"Are you insane? He didn't buy me a Borrelli. I bought that with my hard-earned tips. He bought me a blue polo shirt. It's there somewhere. Hurry up and get him out of there, will ya? Hugh's coming to get me in fifteen minutes."

I couldn't find the polo shirt and declined to remove the Borrelli. I walked downstairs, determined to enjoy the fruits of my brother's alleged hard labor.

"You know what?" I smiled at Antonio. "I'm going to wear this. Then, if you're very good, I'll model the shirt you bought me when we come home."

What the hell was I saying? Boy, I really *was* channeling my cheeky brother.

"Model? And what else will you be wearing?"

"Oh, nothing."

Antonio swallowed hard. "Let's start that part of the evening now."

"No, no, no. You promised me a swim, and I've been looking forward to it."

He stared at me, bursting into laughter.

"Alex, you are so sexy yet . . . such a clown. I love it." He raised himself from the sofa where he'd been leafing through a copy of *Vogue Italia*. "Ready?"

"Sure." I reached across to the sideboard for the car keys. Only local residents were allowed to have cars on the island, so driving one was a complete luxury for me. I was fast supplanting Antonio for Hugh in my fantasy daydream drive.

"You won't be needing those," Antonio said.

"I won't?"

He laughed. "You are so *funny*, Alex. Of course not. We're walking, remember?"

Walking? I plotted my brother's early demise as we

stepped outside. "I thought I'd drive us in the Triumph," I said.

"No . . . don't be ridiculous. But now, *bello*, we have to hurry, the tour leaves in five minutes."

He grabbed my hand. Tour? What tour?

We ran down the eighty-eight steps, Antonio holding my hand, dragging me with him. We reached the piazza, and he checked his watch. I checked my heart rate. I was dismayed to learn we were joining a walking tour of the Via Krupp, an ancient, zigzagging road that wove all the way down to the sea. The road had been closed for thirty years until a recent revamp.

The group that congregated outside Café Luxe chatted excitedly. Some had backpacks, but they were backpackers with bucks. Nothing on Capri was cheap. We all exchanged greetings and began to walk toward the starting point of the tour, the delightful Gardens of Augustus.

Some of the group members raved about how the tour would take three hours. *Three hours!*

I suddenly understood why my lovely twin had given me the date with Antonio. He was about as interested in walking as I was. I glanced inside my dad's restaurant as we passed by. He always reopened very late on Sundays after a lengthy siesta. I wasn't sure what I expected, but there were no signs of life. Maybe I'd hoped Alex was in there so I could give him a black eye.

My shoes began to hurt before we even got to the gardens.

Antonio nudged me. "Look, Alex. Aren't they magnificent?"

"Yeah. Magnificent."

A magnificent blister had started to form on the back of my heel. I stifled any complaints since everybody else seemed to be having such a good time. And besides, I was supposed to be my brother. I couldn't blow this date for him on account of a blister.

Why the hell couldn't the damn Via Krupp stay closed forever?

The gardens were spectacular. Little fountains popping from circular ponds bubbled. I hobbled.

We walked down the sharply turning road, admiring the view of the ocean and the other side of Capri, sparkling in the late afternoon sun. I could smell all kinds of herbs. Tiny, dark-headed blackcaps chirped all around us as they hopped from one berry bush to the next.

They're laughing at me. The little bastards.

Everybody else laughed and talked. A few contemplated the wildflowers growing on either side of the zigzagging road. I contemplated the life mystery of how a little thing like a blister on your foot could render you feeling helpless and miserable with pain.

"You know, Alex, I'm a little disappointed in you," Antonio said.

"Oh really?" *Cool! Let's go back!*

"Yes. I mean, how could you even think I'd go to Naples without you? Our whole plan was to go together. I can't wait. You really think your brother will fill in for you this weekend?"

This weekend? I stifled a groan. I covered for Alex most weekends. I wondered when he'd planned to ask me to cover the weekend of the Naples trip, then I wondered if he might have forgotten about it.

"Sure he will. Zeca is a cool guy."

"He's kind of boring, *bello*. Nothing like you."

Boring? He thinks I'm boring? "No, he's not. He's fascinating."

"Fascinating?" Antonio laughed. "You are so funny. You're the one who always says he is . . ."

"Fascinating?"

He laughed. "No . . . *stupido*."

13

"He's not stupid, and just so you know, his cock is much bigger than mine."

"Really? Then it must be huge. Yours is spectacular, you know."

I gaped at him. When had he seen Alex's cock? So much for their *just-kissing* dates. Holy cow, the guy would be expecting sex tonight for sure.

Sweat beaded on my face and neck. Antonio's hand moved to the small of my back. "Are you all right? You look like you're in pain."

"My foot. I have a blister."

He shook his head. "You wore the wrong shoes." He gave my ass a comforting pat and walked ahead of me. He started asking some of the male tourists if they had a spare pair of socks. One of the Swedish men dug into his backpack and handed over a balled-up pair of white athletic socks that gave off a whiff of bleach. At least I knew they were clean. I was touched that Antonio went to so much trouble for me and even handed the Swede some euros in exchange for the socks.

"Don't be silly," Antonio said when I thanked him.

He propped me against a rock as the others kept walking. He removed my left shoe, examining the back of my foot.

"I have a Band-Aid in my medicine kit," the Swede said, walking back toward us, handing it over as if it were a precious metal. In my current state, it was.

"Thank you," I said. "Please, come to my restaurant tomorrow night for dinner, as my guest."

"Really?" The Swede looked ecstatic. "I am on my honeymoon . . ." He indicated a pretty blonde smiling at us from a short distance.

"Both of you," I said. "I'm very grateful."

"Which restaurant is it?" he asked.

"Oh, Café Toppy."

"Yes, I've seen it. Next to the chocolate shop?"

I nodded.

"We would love that, thank you."

As soon as the Swede's back turned, Antonio kissed the top of my foot. It was the most romantic gesture I could ever remember. He opened the Band-Aid and placed it gently over the blister, smoothing down the edges. He rolled the sock up my foot, and I felt my cock hardening inside my jeans. He dropped a kiss on my crotch.

"You are in a feisty mood tonight," he said, grinning as he put the other sock on my right foot and put my shoes on my feet.

What the hell is this guy like in the sack? He's got me rockin' and reeling here just touching my feet!

"You know, I would love to join your little dinner party tomorrow night," he said as we caught up with the others.

My feet felt so good I would have agreed to an organ donation at that point. "Of course," I said. "You're my hero."

He kissed my mouth, and I felt even better.

"You've never invited me to dinner at the restaurant before," he said. He seemed really happy. Technically speaking, I hadn't invited him, but I could hardly have said no. I started to worry just a little that Alex would have a meltdown about it. What if he had plans with the other guy?

I brushed these thoughts away as we approached the marina at the bottom of the cliff. The three extraordinary Faraglioni rocks, the most famous natural formations in Capri, greeted us. In the months I'd been here, I was still mesmerized by the spectacular scenery and the limestone cliffs of the mountainous island that seemed to plunge into the Tyrrhenian Sea. The image changed day by day, hour by hour, depending on the sun's position. What remained a constant was its raw, natural beauty.

I noticed people stripping to their swimsuits and jumping into the water. I was so eager to make a better impression on my hot date that I showed off, swan diving into the crystal blue waters from a jagged cliff edge.

Giving a smiling Antonio a little wave, I took off, arms extended, and — *pow*!

A massive belly flop.

I heard everyone's collective gasp, but I kept a fake smile on my face as I rose to the water's surface, and a few people laughed.

To say it hurt is like saying Kilimanjaro is a hill. I limped back to the pebbly shore in mortal agony.

"You are such a comedian tonight," Antonio said.

My whole body ached. I concentrated on breathing, and as he frolicked in the water, I gingerly felt up my ribs. Nothing seemed broken, thank God. I could just see me powering around the café on the morning shift with a broken rib poking out of my chest. I took a deep breath and moved my hand down to my foot. The Band-Aid was still there. I relaxed a little, but the initial shock of pain lingered. My chest tingled and burned.

"You're all red. Did you hurt yourself with that crazy dive?" Antonio asked, coming toward me with a towel.

I nodded, still winded and fresh out of *bon mots*.

He shook his head. "What's gotten into you tonight?"

Everybody started to walk back. I tried to keep a smile on my face and attempted to distract Antonio from my eternal goofdom by asking him some questions. "So, how was your day today? What did you do?"

He looked surprised. "Is that a joke? You know what I was doing."

For the first time, he seemed annoyed.

Holy crap! What the hell does he do all day? "Well," I said. "I thought —"

"Did you call Teresa and remind her about Sunday?"

I must have adopted my best deer-in-the-headlights expression because he emitted a frustrated *tsk* sound. Whipping out his cell phone, he pressed some numbers.

"Honestly, you had *one* thing to do, Alex. I've arranged everything else . . . Hello, Teresa?" His face split into a handsome, happy grin.

Okay, so what did this guy do for a living? I'd had tragically poor taste in men up until now. God, I hoped he wasn't a bad guy. He didn't look like a hitman, and I hadn't heard about any burglaries. Was he a cop? Nope . . . that didn't fit either. He was way too hot. We had a small police force in Capri, and I knew most of the officers by sight. Besides, Antonio exuded a dangerous air, and I was certain he had a glamorous, exciting job.

I kept trying to figure out what he did for a living, wondering how I could get him to talk when he started to laugh.

"Oh, he called you already? It's all arranged? *Eccelente!*"

He reached over and hugged me. The slight pressure on my body made every fiber of my being ache.

"Am I hurting you?" He frowned. "My poor baby. I thought you forgot all about Teresa and you didn't. And now you are hurting. Come, we go have a little cocktail, some dinner . . . Doctor Antonio will take care of all your troubles."

Was he a doctor? I didn't think so. However, he sure cured all my ailments with his sweet attentiveness. I had no idea who Teresa was, and I guessed it didn't really matter since it was Alex who'd be spending the weekend in Naples with him, not me. Dang. Why did the idea of that bother me so much?

"You feel like pizza?" He put his arm around me. "Would you like to go to Aurora?"

"Aurora? I've never been there. I'm dying to taste their bread."

He pulled back, looking askance at me. "What are you

talking about? We were there last week."

Shit, shit, shit!

I assumed what I hoped was a dignified expression. "Antonio, when I'm with you, I forget where I am and even who I am."

"That's *such* a nice thing to say, Alex . . . or is it Zeca?"

I laughed a little too hard and long, but he looked pink with happiness. I remembered that Alex said I should laugh at the man's jokes. And I did.

Why did he make a joke like that? I worried about this until our food arrived.

Over the best pizza I had ever eaten on the island, we talked about everything under the sun—except what he did for a living. He was a wonderful raconteur. I yearned to know more about him. I wanted to ask about his childhood, his favorite toys . . . I shook my head. This wasn't for me to know. It was Alex's domain. A sense of sadness washed over me. I liked this guy. Why couldn't I meet somebody like him?

"Why so sad, *bello*?" His slipped his arm around me again.

"The pizza's all gone," I said, making a face.

He threw his head back and laughed.

I adored his laughter. It was genuine and deep. It was also quite contagious.

"You want more?" he asked.

I hesitated a fraction of a moment.

"*Bello*," he said. "You only have to ask. I will give you anything you want."

"Anything?"

His gaze seared into mine. "Anything."

"Then I would love the margherita. Do you mind?"

"No, I don't mind." He had a funny expression on his face. "You told me you hated it last time."

"Er . . . um . . ."

"Wow . . . you are full of surprises tonight." He beckoned the waiter and ordered more pizza. "Would you like some more coffee?"

I nodded. To me, coffee and pizza should be their own special food group. I reached across the table for the last piece of bread still languishing in the basket. The restaurant's specialty was the bread, which was plain, baked pizza dough brushed with a little olive oil. My cell phone rang. I glanced at the readout.

"It's my dad. I have to take this. I'm sorry."

Antonio waved off my apologies. "You've been great tonight. You haven't been . . ." He imitated two thumbs texting madly. Boy, he had my brother nailed.

He pulled out his own phone. "Maybe I should check my messages too. Maybe I'll take a leak."

He leaned over and kissed me as I took the call.

"Hey, Dad." I grinned at Antonio. "Don't be too long."

He pretended to hurry away from the table, turning to grin at me.

My father screamed down the phone. "Zeca!"

"Yes, Dad?"

"What the hell did you do to my car?"

"I didn't touch your car."

"Yes, you did. Your brother told me he let you borrow it. And it's sinking to the bottom of the bloody sea!"

CHAPTER TWO

It was hard to shake off my hot, handsome, horny date, but I had to meet my father and brother at the family home.

"My brother crashed Dad's car, his Triumph. I need to go home and, um . . . mediate."

Antonio seemed surprised. "Didn't he just get that car?"

"Yep, two weeks ago."

"Well." He paused. "I can't say I'm not disappointed, but you should go help your brother. That Zeca. You're always cleaning up his messes."

My messes? I was so angry that even one of Antonio's delicious kisses couldn't cheer me up. I was mad until I reminded myself I could easily suffocate my brother as he slept. No muss, no fuss.

"Don't look so sad," Antonio said. "I didn't mean to spoil our beautiful evening."

"It *was* beautiful." I leaned into him for a kiss. He was a passionate kisser. I fully entertained the notion of nude romping with him. Too bad it was only a fantasy.

"At least I get to see you tomorrow night," he said.

I smiled. Yes, we'd be together the following evening when he came to the restaurant for dinner. *Oh God . . . I'll be waiting on him and Alex.*

He walked all the way up the eight-hundred-plus stairs with me, gave me a kiss that curled my toes and officially gave me the worst case of blue balls on record. I winced when he held me a little too tightly.

"Are you okay?" he asked me. "You and your brother

aren't always this accident-prone, are you?"

I laughed. He shook his head.

My father's shrieking voice pierced the soft, moonlit sky.

"Zeca, you lousy, good-for-nothing shit. Get in this house now!"

"Oh my God, he's talking to your brother like that?"

"Yes," I said, sweat breaking out on my skin yet again on our date.

"I'm afraid to leave you two with him. Maybe I should come with you."

"No, no, I'll be fine. I'll call you when he's calmed down."

He hesitated. "You're sure?"

He looked very disturbed, and my dad was now at the window screaming again. My brother appeared beside him, looking stricken.

"Why does he keep looking at you?" Antonio asked.

"I'm the mediator. They need me."

Antonio seemed to accept this. I gave him a finger wave and rushed inside, missing the last thing Antonio said to me. Inside the house, I tried to keep my voice down in case Antonio was still outside but my dad raged at me.

"How could you take my bloody car and hoon around town in it and let it just roll down the bloody mountain into the sea?"

I opened my mouth, but he just kept screaming, jabbing me in the chest.

"Dad," I said, really not wanting the entire neighborhood to hear me getting reamed for something I didn't do. I also didn't want my dad to have a heart attack. He'd turned a shade of purple that might be fetching on an eggplant, but not a middle-aged man. Alex stood beside him, a bizarre look on his face I couldn't quite read.

The front door blew open. It was Antonio.

"Look, Mr. Colombo, I can't have you screaming at Alex

this way. He's been with me all night. Why are you blaming *him*?"

Oh my God.

My father gaped at him. "Who the fuck are you?"

"Antonio Moretti. I'm Alex's boyfriend."

"Oh right, right." Dad looked rattled.

Antonio stuck his paw out. He and my dad shook hands.

Alex ran a hand over his face. For the first time in his life, my brother looked unnerved.

Dad was in a quieter mood now. "I'm sorry for the shouting," he said. "You're right. I shouldn't blame . . . Alex."

Dad knows. He's figured out that I didn't drive the car.

Antonio's threatening expression relaxed a little.

"I need to talk to my sons," Dad said. "Alone."

"Are you okay?" Antonio asked me. I nodded.

"Call me before you go to sleep, okay? I'll see you tomorrow." He flicked an angry glance at my brother and father and left.

This time, in the chilling silence that ensued, I heard him running down the steps back to the piazza.

"Mind telling me what the fuck is going on?" Dad looked at Alex.

Alex opened his mouth.

Dad held up a hand. "You two have been switching identities again." To me, he said, "Zeca, obviously it was your brother behind the wheel. When I get mad, I lose all reason." He shook his fist at Alex. "You went on letting me think it was Zeca!"

"It's his fault," Alex said.

"How's it *my* fault?"

"You were supposed to take the car. I had a few drinks and . . ." He shrugged.

"The cost of the retrieval and all the repairs are coming out of your pocket," my father said to Alex, who fumed. "You killed my new car!" He stomped out of the house.

Alex stared at the floor.

"I have a few more bones to pick with you," I said.

"Not now."

"You made up a bunch of bullshit about me to Antonio, who, by the way, is a wonderful man. He's crazy about you."

"Oh save it."

"No, I won't save it. He's a sweet guy. He deserves better than . . . being duped."

"Yeah, I know. He's sweet but —"

"He's coming to dinner at the restaurant tomorrow night."

"What? He can't do that! Hugh's coming there."

"Too bad. Take him somewhere else."

"But —"

"No buts. He's coming to the restaurant with a Swedish couple who helped me on the bloody walk you were supposed to be on."

He grinned then. "Was it fun?"

"Fuck you! And, by the way, he's taking you to Naples for the weekend and don't forget about Teresa on Sunday."

"Teresa?" His nose scrunched in confusion. "Oh, her. Yeah. Right."

"I still have no idea what Antonio does for a living. You got any idea?"

My brother's laugh was nasty. "Why do you care? He's not your boyfriend. He's *my* boyfriend."

"Right. It's best you remember that before you blow him off again. Tonight was really embarrassing. Especially since you keep telling him I'm stupid, boring and, oh yeah, you're constantly cleaning up my messes."

He stared at me. "Shit. You're wearing my Borrelli."

"Oh fuck off," I said, and stomped to my room.

All night I tossed around in my normally very comfy bed. I awoke every hour, it seemed. My arms ached. The cappuccino machine at the restaurant was an old one, very prized in the coffee world but hard on the arms. You had to press the metal and wood arms up and down to make the coffee. It was quite a workout, but my arms always ached first thing in the morning, not after a long day at work, which constantly surprised me.

At dawn, out of sheer frustration, anger and restlessness, I left my room. My brother's door was wide open. He was on his bed, sprawled on the covers fully clothed, his two cell phones twinkling beside him, his laptop tottering on the edge of his bed. I grabbed it and put it on his dresser.

I looked outside his windows. Nightlights still dotted the mountainside, as if deranged fairies had sprinkled an overabundance of stardust willy-nilly. I could see lights way up in the mountains. Where were they coming from? Who lived up there? Were they in caves? There was still so much for me to explore on this tiny, yet ever-expanding island.

Brushing aside fantasies of exploring it with Antonio, I tried not to think of his hot peppery kisses across my jawline. God, he was a passionate man.

Pending dawn was turning the sky a beautiful shade of deep blue. All the stars gracing the sweep of sky I could see indicated it was going to be a gorgeous day. I detected movement and saw an old lady a few houses away, sweeping outside her door.

I went downstairs, switching on lights as I went. In the kitchen, there was a tiny stub of cinnamon bread left for me. I snatched it up, threw the lid off the butter urn and slathered some on the bread, swallowing it in two bites.

Hunting around for more food, I found a loaf of Angelina's thyme and lemon bread hidden in the potato barrel. The other men in my family had to work a lot harder to hide the good stuff from me. I cut a few thick slices of bread whilst I waited for the coffeemaker to do its thing. Slathering a heavy layer of lemon butter on the bread, I took my breakfast to the sofa. I picked up the magazine on the coffee table, smiling at the thought that Antonio had held it in his hands the previous evening.

The smile fled from my face. I liked the guy. I'd sneaked in so many kisses and enjoyed his thoughtful glances, his warm and constant touch. Damn. I could fall for him. It burned me to know that Alex didn't realize how awesome the guy was. I threw the magazine back on the coffee table, drained my coffee and took my last remaining slice of bread to work with me. I always got the ball rolling in the mornings at Café Toppy. I was disappointed nobody materialized with lemony tidbits, but it was still early. I made it to work before the sun even emerged in the sky.

As was my wont, I opened all the glass-fronted doors that opened and closed like shutters around the café. I swept the floors, which I always did, in spite of the fact, somebody would have swept the night before. I turned on the cappuccino machine, letting it warm up. I checked the levels of our iced coffee, iced tea, and iced chocolate jugs and began the process of preparing food for the day.

Toppy's might have the name "café" in its title, but it was a restaurant. The kitchen in back was equipped to feed sixty people at a time. Alex and I took turns working the front bar, which had the coffee machine and a series of low fridges behind the counter. It also had a small sink in which to wash cups and glasses. Plates and utensils other than teaspoons were handled in the main kitchen.

I wiped down the frothing tools on the gigantic cappuccino machine. My arms still ached. They always ached lately, and I had no idea why. I should have been used to the damn machine by now. I checked all the coffee cups for lipstick marks, made sure I had plenty of teaspoons and then turned on the iPod. I selected Cecilia Bartoli, a beloved Italian opera singer. I adored her album *Se Tu M'ami — If You Love Me* — a collection of eighteenth-century Italian love songs. Her beautiful mezzo-soprano voice always lifted my spirits. Her rendition of "Caro Mio Ben" — "My Dear Beloved" — is exquisite. Alex almost caused a traffic accident the first time we heard it driving around Rome in our rental car upon our arrival in Italy. We played it over and over again.

My thoughts strayed to Antonio. I felt like the person in the song, sad to think of a life without this man's love. I forced myself not to think about him. He was Alex's boyfriend, not mine.

Remember that, dumbass, and don't accept another date with him again, no matter what Alex says.

I sighed as I put fresh lemon leaves in the tabletop vases, pleased that our yellow roses next to them were still holding strong. Yellow roses meant friendship, someone had told me, and also betrayal. I felt guilty about my part in last night's date. I tried to rationalize that I'd been a fun, attentive date in spite of my blister and the stupid belly flop. I remembered Antonio's ardent kisses and wanted to crawl into my bed until I was eighty. Let life pass me by. I would have to watch Alex chew up and spit out Antonio. It was what he always did.

"Hey there," a voice said.

I smiled and returned the greeting.

Chris Acton was a British actor who'd worked with my dad on his soap opera back in England. He'd developed a huge ego — Chris's description, not mine — and quit the show thinking he'd be flooded with film offers. When he wasn't, he hit the road and traveled through Europe with his earnings. He'd been in Capri for a week and seemed a bit aimless to me. He gravitated toward Toppy as if he was some kind of grounding force, a life preserver — a grave mistake in my opinion since my dad was a beautiful nutcase. Chris came to breakfast at the café every morning.

Casting a critical eye on everything, I liked what I saw. I picked up my order pad and rushed to his side.

"I'll just have the usual," he said.

Boy was he lucky he got me. Alex would have been sarcastic. I could hear him now. *Your usual what?*

I nodded, wrote out the order for cappuccino and a Greek omelet and raced back behind the counter. The coffee machine was ready. I made the cappuccino first. I had never told anybody that I had a recurring nightmare, which was that on a busy day I would make the wrong coffees, lattés instead of cappuccinos. Or vice versa.

Teaspoons. They were my other nightmare. Running out of them. That was a *big* nightmare. I handled stress pretty well, I thought, dealing with the London Stock Exchange and frantic people fretting about their money. Nothing, however, beat dealing with people who wanted a cup of coffee. Café Toppy was either dead or slammed. There was no middle ground.

I raced to the table with Chris's cappuccino and tore into the kitchen to make his omelet. The bread arrived at the back door as I beat the eggs. I thanked the delivery guy, a cuter one than usual. I knew that Chris liked his bread toasted lightly. He was ready for his second cup of coffee by the time I delivered his food. I made him the second cappuccino and was taking it to him when I saw Antonio lounging in the doorway.

"Hi," I said. I became an instant mess. I caught Chris's curious glance as I slopped coffee into the saucer. *Damn.*

"Have you met one another?" I asked.

Antonio blinked, and I introduced them. The two men started chatting, and Antonio took a seat beside Chris. My hand shook as I took a paper towel over to Chris and blotted his saucer.

"Would you like a cup of coffee?" I asked Antonio. I stopped my hand from falling to his shoulder just in time. I was myself now. Zeca couldn't touch him.

"Thanks, Zeca," he said.

I turned and made him a cappuccino, willing myself not to do something stupid with it before I could get it to him. I gave him extra foam, the way I'd heard him ask the waiter for it the previous night, and took it to the table. He and Chris were still engaged in animated conversation. I removed the coffee holders from the machine, emptying them into the plant container under the counter.

Antonio came over to me, and I offered him my brightest smile.

He held up his cup.

"Is something wrong?" I asked.

He dipped his spoon into his cup and lifted it out. An entire paper napkin was in it. How the hell had that happened?

"Oh my God. I'm so sorry. I'll make you another one."

"No problem . . . thanks. I appreciate it." He hesitated as I scooped fresh coffee into the holder. "Any idea what time Alex will be here?"

"I'm expecting him here around noon."

He nodded. "I tried calling him, but he doesn't answer."

"Maybe he's still asleep."

He said something I couldn't hear over the whooshing of the cappuccino machine. I handed the cup back to him.

"Thanks, Zeca."

He drifted back to the table, and his discussion with Chris continued. I was so jealous I wanted to spit. I caught snatches of their conversation, heard the words "music" and "Naples." If I hadn't known Chris was straight, I might have hurled the coffee machine at his head.

The restaurant started to fill quickly. I had a table of eight that took up my time, and I started to stress but hoped it didn't show. Antonio asked for his check, but I waved it off. Chris had left his euros under his knife like he usually did.

"Will you be here tonight?" Antonio asked me, peeling off a couple of bills. This time I touched his arm.

"Please don't. It was my pleasure."

He nodded. "Thanks. So, will you be here?"

"Possibly." I had no idea, actually.

He lifted his shoulders. "I'll see you when I see you then."

I found Chris strolling out of the can, a lemon-flavored toothpick in his teeth.

"Did you enjoy talking to Antonio?"

He grinned. "Absolutely, what a fascinating guy."

I wanted to ask more, but my tableful of tourists was calling me.

Damn. I picked up my order pad again, and I was off and running.

I was good and tired by the time my siesta hour arrived. I staggered up the stone stairs to the house. It was as if my usual ladies had ganged up on me and decided I was not to receive any more special tidbits. Not even a drop of limoncello to ease my climb.

Inside, I took a long, cool shower, threw on some fresh boxer briefs and dropped to my rumpled bed. I fell into instant sleep and awoke only when Alex shook me.

"You have to come to the restaurant."

"Why?"

"You invited Antonio and the Swedes, and I can't be in two places at once."

"Oh no," I said. The last thing I wanted was to work all evening, watching as Antonio kissed and cuddled my brother.

"I thought you liked Antonio?" Alex asked.

"What's that got to do with anything?"

"He's all excited about tonight, thanks to you."

I did get a moment of pleasure out of his irritated expression. "Well, that's great. Right?"

He frowned.

"It's my night off," I reminded him. *I knew this would happen. This is a nightmare. Holy fuck. Next, I'll be running out of teaspoons.*

"You're the one who organized this little dinner party!"

"You're the one who asked me to masquerade as you. Forgive me for trying to make you out to be a gracious, nice guy."

He put his hands to his hips, another classic, unattractive trait he inherited from Toppy.

"Look," he said, surprising me by acting calm, "I'll stay and do the dishes afterward, okay?"

"No, you won't. You'll go home with him."

"I can't go home with him. I have a date with Hugh right after dinner." He held up his hands. "I promise to come back and clean up the mess. I'll even tell Dad."

Yeah, right.

For some reason, I said yes. I threw on some clean clothes, and we walked back down to the piazza. I examined my feelings and didn't much like what I saw. I realized I wanted to see Antonio.

"Do you like Antonio?" I asked Alex.

"Sure, he's nice. Damn good kisser."

"You can say that again."

He stopped on the stairs. "Why's that crazy lady from next door leaning out the windows, waving at me?"

I bit my lip, amused. I wasn't quite ready to tell him yet. Let him suffer her unwanted attentions for a while.

"Yoo-hoo!" she shrieked, waving madly.

He gave her a finger wave, shook his head, and returned his attention to our conversation, glaring at me belatedly.

"Hey," I reminded him, "I was being you. I had to kiss him. I couldn't act as if kissing him was disgusting, you know."

Alex resumed his descent. "You're right."

"Are you looking forward to the weekend in Naples?"

"I guess."

"You guess? You don't sound very certain."

"It's Hugh's last weekend in town. I'm kinda conflicted, truth be told." He stopped again. "You may as well know, I'm planning to cancel the weekend in Naples. Hugh wants to take me to Portofino."

Portofino was certainly an idyllic spot for lovers. Frankly, I would have gone anywhere Antonio asked me to go. It was with a heart bound by burdensome emotions that I spotted him waiting at the bottom of the stairs. His smile was strong and warm. My brother stepped easily into his arms and kissed him.

I kept smiling, walking past them, realizing I had it bad for Antonio. He and Alex ran past me, holding hands and laughing.

It took all my resolve not to turn and run. I knew I had it bad because I realized I wasn't doing this for Alex. I was doing this for Antonio.

CHAPTER THREE

I leaned against the cappuccino machine and watched Antonio kissing Alex. They'd worked their way through a three-course meal. Our evening waiters, two locals who worked Friday and Saturday nights and the odd weeknight Toppy called them in, handled the table, but I did plenty too. And it killed me.

The Swedish tourist was an anthropologist, which fascinated me. He'd conducted a twelve-year study of children living in the inner city of Naples, a subject Antonio seemed to find as absorbing as I did. I hated leaving the table and kept finding excuses to be there.

An old episode of *I Love Lucy* flashed in my mind, where Lucy pretends to be Ethel's maid, and instead of enjoying a visit with the Mertzes' long-lost vaudeville buddy, Lucy is waiting on him hand and foot.

The Swedish couple left, thanking me for my attentive services. I cringed, hoping I hadn't been a buttinsky, while Alex and Antonio lingered over coffee and limoncello.

Watching their playful interaction was like crawling on my hands and knees over crushed glass. I was determined never, *ever* to impersonate my brother again. For three and a half hours, I'd endured their laughter, their shared whispers . . . I had to bite my tongue and not laugh as Antonio described my belly flop to Dad, who was now sitting with them. He thought it was funny. Only Alex remained silent.

He walked over to me at the coffee machine.

"You belly flopped? Man, you're such an idiot."

"Thanks, you too."

He laughed then stole a glance over his shoulder, but Antonio was in deep discussion with Dad.

His voice dropped. "Listen, I gotta go meet Hugh. I'll walk out with Antonio. I'll kiss him goodnight and talk to him. Just get everything into the kitchen and leave it there."

"You can bet your last euro I'll do that," I said.

Antonio came and said goodbye, thanking me for the wonderful meal. "Toppy tells me you personally made the pumpkin and pesto pizza we had for our appetizers."

I was so afraid of grabbing his face and sticking my tongue down his throat that I grabbed one of the coffee holders on the cappuccino machine and cleaned it, even though it didn't need it. "Yeah, I did. I hope you enjoyed it."

"Of course I did. It was amazing. Thanks again. I wish you could have joined us."

Me too! "It was my pleasure to serve you."

Our gazes held for a brief moment. Oh, he was a sexy guy. He took off, joining my brother at the door. I watched with a sourness roiling in my belly as I stacked the dishware from the table to take to the kitchen.

"Are you okay, kid?" Dad asked when he saw me.

"Yes, why?"

"I can see you have some feelings for the cop."

"Cop? What cop?"

"Antonio."

"He's a cop?"

"You didn't know?"

I shook my head. Man . . . he had to be about the sexiest man I'd ever seen—even in the movies. A cop. It sort of fit. The air of danger, the smart, hidden-secret eyes. Oh, his eyes! "How come I haven't seen him at the police station or in a uniform?"

"Alex didn't tell you?"

"No." I found myself rinsing and stacking dishes in the washer, out of habit.

"Aren't you supposed to leave those for Alex?"

"No. I can do it. Dad, what didn't Alex tell me about Antonio?"

"He busted a big drug ring in Naples. As you know, the city has its charms *and* its seamy underbelly. It's completely controlled by the Camorra, the mafia. And he busted the wrong ring. He got a slap on the wrist and was sent here to work the Capri Tourism office."

Ouch. Oh man. No wonder he had a weird reaction when I asked what he did all day. I could just imagine the dumbass stuff he had to deal with—missing sunglasses, passports, lost visitors. For a guy who'd busted a major drug ring, it had to be a huge comedown.

Dad wiped the tables out front and started putting up the chairs.

"You want a little limoncello?" he called out to me.

"Sure."

We sat and downed our first glass. We slowly sipped the second. He'd locked all the doors that normally opened out onto the piazza. It was just me and Dad. It was often just the two of us at closing time. I'd come to enjoy our last evening drink before he raced off to his breathless widow and I went home to my dreams.

"How is Angelina?" I asked.

I expected his usual answer of, "Oh, she's gorgeous," but this time he surprised me.

"Well," he said, "I don't know."

"What's that supposed to mean?"

"She's acting kind of funny."

"Funny how?"

"She says she wants the night off. She wants space. Can you believe it?"

"Sure I can."

He gaped at me. "How can you say that?"

I blew out a sigh. I knew what the problem was. My dad is like a gale-force wind in his relationships. He's inclined to smother his partners. I should know because it's one of the least attractive traits I've inherited from him.

When I suggested he give her the time she craves and even back off a little, he stuck out his bottom lip in thought.

"Antonio said the same thing."

"You asked Antonio's advice on your love relationship?"

Dad shrugged. "He's a cop. I figured it was more entertaining for him to listen to than people's stories of missing beach umbrellas."

Oh geez. "So, you have it from both of us now. Leave her alone, and she'll come running. You'll see."

"Yeah, I guess."

Mr. Pampina, our neighbor who thought that I'd been gawking at his wife from Alex's bedroom the night before, tapped at one of the doors. Dad threw it open then turned to me.

"Want to come out for drinks, Zeca?" he asked me.

The truth was, I was tired, but I also didn't want to be home alone. "Sure," I said.

"I was kidding." Dad rolled his eyes. "I was just being polite. I'm gonna go hang out with the guys for a while. See you back at the house."

"Yeah, okay." Now I felt really stupid. *God, maybe I really am pathetic. I can't tell a fake invitation from a real one.*

I washed the glasses, swept the floors, turned off the lights and sat behind the counter. Watching people walk by arm in arm was like viewing a moving postcard of Capri. I listened to Cecilia Bartoli singing "Caro Mio Ben" again.

Ugh. I hated the thought of Alex and Antonio kissing somewhere scenic. *Hey,* I reasoned with myself, *someplace beautiful that doesn't involve a bedroom is preferable to the alter-*

native. I dreaded their wild weekend of sex in Naples. Just hated it. The song captured all my anguish, my high dramatic state. On the one hand, my feelings seemed unreal since I hardly knew Antonio. On the other, like the song says, the soul knows what it knows and yearns for what it recognizes.

When I'd listened to it a couple of times, I turned off the iPod, locked up and walked home. I was halfway up the stairs when Alex called me, whispering frantically.

"You have to cover for me."

"When? What do you mean?"

"I can't talk long. Hugh's in the can. I need you to cover for me in Naples this weekend. Antonio got really upset. He went mad when I tried to cancel our date. I can't get out of it. Look, I really want to go to Portofino with Hugh. I think he might really be the one."

"Really?"

My thoughts whirled. I'd had two limoncellos. Man, I was a pretty soft touch after a couple of those. I licked my lips and leaned against the railing of the stairs, holding my cell phone to my ear.

"You still there?" he asked. "I want to go to Portofino. Besides, Naples is supposed to be the most closeted Italian city of them all. I have no idea why Antonio is so hot to go there."

I didn't care how closeted Naples was. I would have gone to any city, anywhere, anytime, to be with Antonio. I thought about his laughter, his gentle mocking way with me, and I could still feel his kisses on my face . . .

"No, I don't think I can, Alex. He's expecting sex, and I can't avoid him for a whole weekend."

"Fuck," he said. I heard kissing sounds.

"You know what?" he said. "Try to resist. If you can't, it's cool. He's a hot guy, I know."

I couldn't tamp down my elation, but boy did I try hard not to show it to my brother. "Okay. So you're not gonna come unglued?"

"Of course not. You're doing me a big favor."

I nodded. Yes, I was. I was doing *me* a big favor too. I wouldn't be able to resist Antonio. Oh, I'd make a modest effort . . . but I wanted to be naked and in bed with him. More than anything else in the world.

"Say," I said, "what is this thing with Teresa in Naples?"

"Oh, I'll explain that later. I gotta go. I got a man with a nice hard cock here just begging for my attention."

I heard an explosion of laughter on the other end of the line.

"Oh, before I go," he said between noisy kisses, "I ran into our next-door neighbor. What's her name?"

"Mrs. Pampina?"

"Uh-huh. She turned up at the front door this morning. She was all over me. Invited me over for coffee. Is that weird or what?"

I stifled my own wild laughter. I longed to say *she thinks you're hot for her*, but he ended the call.

My walk home left me feeling high as a kite, a sensation that had absolutely nothing to do with limoncello. It was the feeling only a budding romance can give you. I sat in my room, looking out the window, and realized I couldn't wait for the weekend. Three whole days to get through before then.

It was early in the morning when depression set in. I didn't think I could go through with it. I couldn't be in bed with Antonio as he screamed out my brother's name in his moment of bliss . . .

I didn't see Antonio again over the next two days, but our

pending departure lingered foremost in my mind, no matter what I was doing. In the brief moments I caught up with Alex, he told me that Antonio would meet me at the café at three on Friday afternoon.

Mrs. Pampina started turning up. At first, Alex seemed surprised, then amused by her apparent obsession. Her dresses got tighter, and we noticed her drifting from one designer boutique to another, buying new things. One morning I spotted her in the shoe store next to our café as I waited on the outdoor tables and she gave me a wink.

When she showed up at the café half an hour later with an armful of couture bags and a massive heart-shaped chocolate box, I heard my brother gasp.

"I'm not here," he hissed, dropping down behind the counter beside me.

"Alex?" she asked, grinning, her cherry-red lipstick covering her teeth.

"He's right here," I said and yanked him to his feet.

But these little victories were hollow. Alex's moments of discomfort could not outweigh mine. The closer the time came to my weekend trip, the more I felt I had to tell Antonio the truth. At the very least, I felt I needed to try to cancel our plans, much as I wanted to go to Naples with him.

Thursday night, I slept badly, my arms inexplicably aching again the next morning. A good hot shower helped a little. At work, I called my father and asked him to come in a little early to mind the café. When he arrived, he seemed upset.

"She wants the night off again," he said, exasperated. "We had the best sex ever last night. What's wrong with the woman?"

"You're too much man for her, Toppy," I said.

He snapped his fingers. "That's exactly what *she* said. Maybe I should . . . I dunno . . . date around a little."

"That's a good idea. Sleep with a couple of her friends. That's a classy thing to do on a small island."

He slapped my arm. "I'm thinking tourists. Maybe a female fan or two."

"Oh my God. You want to bed a groupie?" I'd seen my father's fans. They were middle-aged, frenzied desperadoes. They invaded the island during side trips on package tours of Italy, with old copies of *TV Times* in their hands. One persistent woman even rode to shore in a dinghy from a cruise ship, claiming undying love for my father, who hid in the café restroom. It was the only time Alex, and I had to call the local police and ask them to remove an unruly customer. Now my dad wanted to bed the bewitched? *Whatever.*

I walked to Antonio's office, but it was closed. I wondered briefly if he was with Alex, who hadn't come home the previous night. The thought niggled at me, so I was pleasantly surprised to find Antonio waiting at the café when I returned.

He wore tight, sexy, fly-button jeans and a crisp, form-fitting, navy blue T-shirt over them. I longed to lift the hem and lick the creamy caramel skin of his belly.

We exchanged hot looks, and I saw Dad hovering. He shrugged at me.

"Are you ready?" Antonio asked.

"Ready?" I stared at him in my stupid, fast-becoming-patented way.

"To go to Naples."

My father stared at Antonio, then at me.

"I thought we were leaving at three," I said. "I haven't even had my first cup of coffee yet."

"You're not leaving me alone," my father said.

I felt helpless.

"*Bello,* I called and left you a message on your cell phone. You didn't get it?"

"I didn't check, I'm sorry."

"We have to go early. I have a meeting in Naples. I thought we could still go together and we'll have lunch. Please tell me you can come."

I started to panic. He wouldn't be able to call me all weekend. No matter what he'd be doing, if he left me a message, he had Alex's number, not mine.

"Can you come?" he asked.

"Go," Dad said. "I'll figure it out."

I hesitated. "But, Dad, Friday is hell day."

"I'll get your brother here."

"Isn't Zeca the one who normally opens?" Antonio asked.

"Yes, he is. Why don't you call him, Dad?"

"I will. You get going. Don't keep the man waiting."

I smiled at Antonio. "My bag is packed. It's in the storeroom. You have time for a coffee?"

He checked his watch. "A quick one."

"I'll make it," Dad said, but he followed me to the storeroom. "What the hell is going on? You're going to Naples with him?"

I nodded. "Alex asked me to go."

"This is getting a bit twisted, mate. Are you going to bang him?"

Hopefully. "I don't know, Dad."

"Listen . . . I'm going to say this just once. You're a sweet guy, Zeca. I know your mother . . ." His voice faltered. "I know it was tough for you, and Lord knows I've done my best, but it hurts to see the way you and Alex . . ." He stopped.

"You're a great dad," I said. "Truly."

"Then please listen to me. If this guy is for you, go for it. Don't run from love."

It was a huge speech for my father. It left me stunned.

"Alex? Toppy? Everything okay?" Antonio called out.

Instead of rushing out to make coffee, my dad put his hand on my arm.

"You have to love before you can be relentless, kid. Always remember that."

Back in the café, I was amazed to find my wayward brother making the cappuccinos. I quickly took over.

"You have to give me your cell phone. He can't call me. He left messages," I whispered.

"No way," he ground out. "Hugh has to be able to reach me." He put his mouth to my ear. "Get him out of here. Hugh is on his way."

"You're such an ass, Alex." I took our coffees to the table. I gave Antonio his cappuccino and sipped on mine.

"How is it?" I asked.

"It's missing a little something," he said.

I grinned. "Oh, you mean a napkin?"

He laughed. "Zeca told you about that?"

My smile froze. I was so confused. I had to remember. Yes, Zeca made the coffee. "Yeah, that's Zeca for you."

We drank quickly.

He seemed in an odd mood, very preoccupied, but I assumed it was due to his meeting in Naples. We said goodbye to my brother, who glowered behind the counter, and my father, who made a big deal about waving us off. I'm sure in that moment he thought I was doing a bang-up acting job, channeling my inner Toppy.

We crossed paths with Hugh as we walked to the funicular and I cringed when I saw that he was wearing Alex's Borrelli shirt. If Antonio noticed it, he didn't say anything.

We also passed Mrs. Pampina. She smoothed down the front of the tightest sundress I'd ever seen, primping her lips in a small compact mirror as she tottered along on impossibly high heels. I wondered where she was going, all dressed up like that. I hoped she was off to see my brother. That would make my morning to know he was as uncomfortable as I was.

At the funicular, Antonio slipped on sunglasses and made a few phone calls after paying for our tickets. I carried our overnight bags onto the little train.

In truth, that thing always unnerved me. It rushed down to the sea awfully fast. I kept thinking about my dad's car tumbling into the water. I had no idea where it was now or what was happening with it. We coursed over the bridge toward the sea, past the zigzag road we'd walked on our date.

Antonio snapped off his cell phone. "You okay, *bello*? You seem nervous."

"Yeah."

"What's wrong?"

He was still wearing shades, so his expression was unreadable.

"I'm okay. It's the train."

"The train makes you nervous?"

I gripped the handlebar on the seat in front of me and focused on breathing.

He looked around him, his hand squeezing my leg. "*Bello*," he said, his voice so soft it was hard to hear him with all the laughter and chatting going on, "I wish I could put my arm around you and comfort you, but I can't in broad daylight, not with all these people around."

I nodded. *Don't think. Don't think about it. Don't think about her. You won't crash. We'll make it.*

"You're really frightened." He seemed astonished. I turned my head and closed my eyes so I wouldn't look down. Then I looked out the window and turned my gaze upward. I caught sight of dozens of tourists climbing the side of the mountain on Capri. Hundreds did this every year, making pilgrimages to an ancient cave containing a statue of the Virgin Mary. I'd never been, and a wave of despair washed over me. If I died, I would never get to visit the Holy Mother. I made a vow to God that if he let me live, I'd go and visit her. Often.

"Are you okay?' Antonio asked.

I closed my eyes and breathed. "Please change the subject." I fought off waves of nausea. Man, my hot weekend was already a disaster on wheels.

We arrived at the sea wall, the jet boat already there. I gulped in great gusts of fresh air. I felt his hand on the small of my back as he steered me onboard. I almost felt as if I were a prisoner in his custody, the determined way he pushed me on to the damn boat. We stood toward the back, watching the view as the jet boat skimmed the waves. I looked behind me. I saw Capri sliding away.

I realized with a pang it was the first time I'd left the island for a dirty weekend. I'd gone to Portofino once with my dad and Angelina. I'd even visited the Amalfi Coast with my cousin Serena, who'd visited from London. This was my first little vacation, and the knowledge filled me with a sudden burst of joy.

Antonio bent his head to my ear. "Your color is coming back."

I nodded.

"Did it bring back bad memories?" he asked.

I didn't respond.

His hand moved to my lower back again, and I felt comforted by his gentle rubbing. I longed to be in bed with him, longed to have him kiss me the way we had the other night.

The boat was fast. Twenty-five minutes later, the harbor in Naples was within reach.

I suddenly knew I couldn't handle being here under false pretenses all weekend. I had to stop this. I had to do it. Now.

"Antonio," I blurted, "I can't do this, I'm sorry."

His mouth tightened when I looked at him. He still wore

his sunglasses, but I could read his lips just fine. He was pissed.

"I'm sorry for all the money you spent. I'll get the first boat back to Capri. I'll repay all your expenses."

He didn't say anything. The boat had reached the dock in Naples, and I was mesmerized by the ancient city. We disembarked, and I tried to focus on Antonio, who stood before me, arms folded.

"Look at me," he said.

"I'm looking at you."

He whipped off his sunglasses, and I gasped. I couldn't lie to him anymore. I couldn't look into those beautiful eyes and do anything but confess. He would hate Alex, though. And Alex would hate me forever.

Alex doesn't want him. I do.

"Tell me what is going on."

I put our bags down.

"Are you crazy?" he asked, snatching them up. "This is Naples. It's not even safe for me to leave *you* on a street corner. Theft here is enormous. Now tell me why you want to leave me."

People hurried past, jostling us. Antonio's focus and gaze remained steady, centered me.

"I don't want to leave you."

His mouth quirked into a smile. God, I adored the way he did that. "Ah, so, you don't want to leave me, but you don't want to be with me, either."

I winced. "It's complicated."

The boat's horn sounded, and it left the harbor, heading back to Capri. Dang. I had another hour to wait for the next boat back to the island.

"Make it simple. Explain."

"I can't."

"You can't, or you won't?"

"It's not you . . . it's me."

44

"Oh my God. Are you kidding me?"

"No, I'm not kidding you." I swallowed. "I'm not the guy you think I am."

"Oh," he said, "I know exactly who you are—Zeca."

CHAPTER FOUR

"How did you know it's me?"

He shook his head. "I didn't at first."

I felt shame coloring my cheeks. "When did you figure it out?"

He looked up and down the street. Now I realized he did this a lot. Was it a cop habit? As if he was checking for trouble? His jaw seemed to tighten. I realized he was very angry.

"When you made me the perfect cappuccino."

I stared at him. "Excuse me?"

His chin jutted toward me. "That was the other giveaway. Your unfailing politeness. Your brother, in a million years, wouldn't remember how I like my coffee. He also would never have thought twice about a Band-Aid. You appreciate the details, Zeca. Do you know how good that makes a man feel?"

"I — er —"

"Alex would never have invited the Swedes to dinner the way you did." He gave a slight grin and shook his head. "Nothing about you made sense on our date, but everything about you *felt* right."

I gulped. "Felt . . . right?"

"Zeca, I suspected the switch but didn't think that two normal, grown men would engage in that kind of crap. I realized it was you at your restaurant the morning after our date. I knew something was weird when I stood outside your house and heard your father screaming, but . . . a few minutes alone with you at the restaurant and I knew. The energy between us was real. It was still there."

Yes, it was. I'd felt it too.

He sighed. "Then that night. You were the unhappiest waiter in all of Italy."

"You tortured me by kissing Alex all night."

Another small smile. "His kisses are fake. Yours are not."

"He likes you—"

"Yeah, which was why he tried to blow me off this weekend. I thought I would take great pleasure in exposing your little games, but I don't. I-I can't."

"What now?" I asked. "Do you hate me?"

"Hate you? No, I don't hate you."

"I'm sorry."

"Why are you here?"

It was a fair question, and I owed him the truth. "My brother's with another guy, but he also wants to keep you."

"That's not what I asked. I want to know why *you* are here."

"Because you're the most amazing man I've ever met."

He shook his head. "This is so fucked up."

"I know. I'm so sorry." I hung my head. It was all over now. Maybe it was for the best.

Neither of us said anything for a moment, and he seemed a little less angry now.

"Well, I don't know what else to say." I felt helpless and miserable. "I care for you too much to go through with the charade. I wanted the chance to be with you, and it was selfish. I'm sorry. Maybe . . . maybe one day you could find it in your heart to forgive me and give me, Zeca, a chance to know you."

He didn't say anything. I reached for my bag, still in his grip.

He pulled his hand back. "Just like that, you're going to run off?"

"I—"

"Jesus, Zeca. I couldn't wait to be with you! I changed our plans so we could leave earlier."

"I thought you had a meeting?"

"Yes, I do. But I also want to be with you. I *don't* want to be with your brother."

"You don't?"

"Hell no! Listen, we're here. We want to be together. Let's see if we like each other. You want to do that?"

"I want to throw myself into your arms and kiss you so badly, my stomach aches."

"See, that's the sort of thing your brother would never say. And, by the way, he doesn't kiss me like you do."

He'd already mentioned that. I couldn't hide my big smile then.

"And don't look so happy, Zeca. You'll be making it up to me for a long time."

"In good ways, I hope."

He stared at me, his expression searing my soul. I was certain my toes emitted puffs of smoke the way his gaze blazed through me. "Let's hope that you think so."

"What about Alex?"

He frowned. "What about him?"

"Are you going to call him and tell him you know the truth?"

He snorted. "Hell no. Your brother is such an ass. Promise me you'll never do this again, this switching thing."

"Oh God, no." I stepped forward then. I had to touch him. My hands went to his hard, flat belly and I moved my arms around his waist, my fingertips finally touching his skin as I slipped them under his polo shirt. The contact sent a jolt of chemical dependency through us both.

"Kiss me, quick," he whispered against my mouth. "We're not supposed to do this in public."

48

And I did.

All around us, people rushed wherever they were going. His kiss sealed my promise that I would never impersonate Alex again. The world stood still. I wanted the kiss to go on. I never wanted him to stop kissing me.

"When we get back to Capri, I'll deal with Alex myself," he said, breaking off our embrace. I nodded, missing his mouth already. "And now, we're going to start our weekend adventures, okay?"

"Very okay."

He smiled. "I think I already adore you, Zeca." He turned, and I followed him, falling into step beside him.

"Where are we going?"

"I'm going to take you home."

"You have a home here?"

He nodded, stopping short at a crosswalk. I saw his gaze flicker everywhere, his hand at my back as we merged with the crowd crossing the street. I felt like a puppy. I wanted to jump up and lick his face. He turned and smiled at me.

"We'll have fun, I promise."

"I know we will."

"We're having dinner with the Swedes tonight. I hope that's okay."

"As long as I don't have to share you in bed with them, I don't care what we do."

He laughed. "No, I'm not big on sharing my men."

"How many do you have?"

"I hope just you, Zeca."

"Did you fuck Alex?"

He flicked an annoyed glance at me as we rounded a corner. "Not for lack of trying."

"If things work out between us, will you stop trying?"

"I don't know. Bedding a pair of twins is every man's fantasy, gay or straight."

That made me stop moving. I couldn't do this. No, I could not. He'd said he didn't want my brother, now this.

People swarmed me, swallowing the distance between us. I wanted to run back to the boat dock, but I panicked, thinking he'd find me there.

He found me right where I was standing, instead. His expression looked haunted as he stuck my bag under the arm holding his own case and he cupped the back of my head, drawing my face to his. He kissed me, but it was hard and brief.

"You stupid man. It was a joke."

"When did you try to bed my brother last?"

He laughed then. "Once I knew you'd switched places, all my thoughts were on you." He frowned. "It's been a problem, trying to figure out how to ask you out without upsetting your brother. Now I no longer care about how he feels."

Antonio took my hand. That wasn't unusual in Italy. Even straight men walked down the street hand in hand. Kissing me—twice—in public was huge. I guessed he really liked me. I felt his grip tightening on mine as we crossed over a huge, widely spaced street. I almost stopped dead again, the street was so enchanting. Tree-lined, with fountains and benches in the middle. I got a distinct gay vibe from it.

I saw a street sign, Piazza Bellini, and felt my feet move a little faster as we entered a stone archway and hurried up two flights of worn stone stairs. He dropped the bags, breathing heavily as he fumbled for his key. I pressed myself into him, facing him. He let go of my hand, holding my ass instead, pressing my crotch to his.

It was impossible. I had to kiss him. I reached up, my mouth finding his ready and willing. He dropped his keys.

"You're a very bad man," he whispered. He gasped as I ran my hand across his crotch. He was rock hard. He bent to pick up his keys, unlocked the door, then dropped our bags inside and closed it behind us with his foot. I threw my arms around his neck. Our mouths collided. I could taste Toppy coffee on his tongue and . . . something else. Lemon rind. When had he eaten lemon? I wanted to know everything about this man, what he liked, what he thought, even what he ate.

He lifted me up and held me as our kisses grew fierce. I loved the sounds we were making. I'd never been with such a passionate man. I couldn't imagine what it was going to be like being in bed with him. Our kisses went on, his tongue working against mine. He put me on the dining room table. The room was open and large. I caught a glimpse of vaulted ceilings and shiny parquet floors. I felt a breeze from somewhere, but all I cared about was him.

I pushed him away from me and lifted up his T-shirt, finally placing a kiss on the hard, flat belly rising from his waistband. He went crazy when I ran my tongue across his stomach. He lifted me up again and carried me across the room.

Outside, I heard cars honking, people yelling and laughing, and inside, my brain was doing the same thing. I'd never experienced such peaks and valleys. He took his mouth off my throat as he draped me across the sofa, climbing between my open legs. Our cocks ground against each other, restless, imprisoned in our pants. He stopped kissing me, unbuttoned my shirt and threw it over his shoulder. He licked his lips.

"Man, I don't have time for this."

"God . . . I'm so hard, Antonio. I want you."

"I want you too. Tell me . . . please, tell me I'm not going to come back and find you gone."

"Never. God, do you have to go?"

He smiled; it was a lovely smile. "Yes. I have . . . a disciplinary hearing." He checked his watch. "In twenty minutes."

"So it's true then?"

He looked cagey. "Is what true?"

"You made a big drug bust, and they punished you by sending you to Capri."

He nodded. "Yes, it's true."

"I want . . . I want you to make love to me. We'll both feel better."

He dropped a kiss on my forehead. "I want to wait. I want our first time to be special. Our first time will be forever."

Antonio got up from the sofa. "I want you, Zeca. I promise we'll have the whole weekend together. Tonight I have to share you, but tomorrow, I'm taking you somewhere amazing."

"Where?"

"You'll see."

"I hope this weekend starts with a private tour of your bedroom."

"You'll get that as soon as I come home."

He held out his hand to me and helped me up from the sofa. He quickly showed me around his beautiful loft. "It was my father's love nest. He had a mistress," he said.

"Oh, how Italian."

"When he died, he left it to me."

"Was she pissed?"

He shrugged. "Maybe. I made sure she had a home of her own."

"What about your mother?"

"She got all his money."

He showed me the bathroom, bedroom, and the surprisingly modern kitchen. "There's no food, and I am sorry for that. I imagine you are hungry."

"Now that you've stopped kissing me, I realize I'm

starving."

He checked his watch again. "Zeca, I have to go. There's a very famous café, Scaturchio patisserie, in St. Domenico Maggiore Square. I can show you the way. Do you feel like having some breakfast there, maybe taking a walk?"

"I would love nothing better than to have a cappuccino somebody else has made."

He grinned. "That's another thing. You work five times as hard as your brother."

He'd observed a lot, it seemed. He changed into a white shirt and dark pants. I caught a glimpse of his black boxer briefs and felt a thrill at the monster bulge. He ran a comb through his hair.

"How do I look?"

"Perfect."

He leaned forward and kissed me. "You are good for my ego."

"Can I walk to your hearing with you?"

He shook his head. "I need to clear my head, gather my thoughts. You make me fall apart, in beautiful ways, but I like knowing you're here, waiting for me. You need to give me your cell phone number so I can contact you."

I gave it to him, and he put it into his phone. He scribbled out his address for me. He gave me a large iron key for the door, and we went back downstairs. I felt seriously deprived after our make-out session. My cock and balls felt awfully uncomfortable in my jeans. I was walking funny, and he hadn't even done anything to me yet.

In a hidden alcove between two of the archways at the front of his building, he pinned me against the wall and kissed me.

We walked a couple of blocks, and he pointed out the elegant-looking patisserie.

"They are known for their *sfogliatella*. Their rum *babas* are my personal favorite."

"And their coffee?"

"I happen to be involved with a man who makes the best coffee in the world, so I'm inclined to pooh-pooh their efforts."

I laughed then. He was adorable.

"Zeca, I must leave you. It's temporary, but I must go."

"Good luck," I said.

"Thanks."

"There's so much I want to ask you," I said.

He gave me one more kiss. "And I, you. If you want to go home, I'll find you." He lifted his hand, his knuckles grazing my chin. I knew he wanted to kiss me again. We stared at one another, the heat flaring between us.

"Will you be okay, Antonio?"

His gaze stayed on my face. "They took everything away from me. There's nothing left that they can take." His smile was small. Sad but sweet.

"I wish you would let me come with you. I want to be close to you."

"You will be." He took my shoulders and spun me around, his mouth at my ear.

"See that building there?"

He pointed to what looked like an ancient, beautiful stone building.

"I'll be right there. I can look out the window and see you. I want you to buy some coffee and pastries. Have fun, relax."

"Don't worry, I will," I said, turning again.

He looked up and down the street.

"*Bacio*," he requested. I kissed him quickly, his gaze darting around, and with that, he was gone.

I walked into Scaturchio and almost swooned. The sights and smells of the place were incredible. I studied the menu.

The bakery was a hundred years old, so they had to know their stuff. I ordered a *sfogliatella*, a delicious-looking flaky pastry made with ricotta cheese and orange water. I ordered a café latté and sat across the street at one of the many tables on the pebbled promenade. The people parade consumed me as I just about licked my plate clean. The coffee was a lot better than Antonio had suggested. An hour slipped by, and I walked back into the bakery, ordered another coffee and a *baba*. It came with a swirl of pastry cream on top of it, and I even licked my fork when I was done. Twice.

Two hours had gone by, and I'd had no word from Antonio. I worried about what they were doing to him. I strolled the neighborhood, drinking it all in. In ancient times, our part of southern Italy had been dominated by the Emperor Tiberius, whose cruel reach extended beyond Naples even to Capri. He was known to become displeased with his subjects at the drop of a hat and pushed dozens of them off cliffs to their deaths. I shook such maudlin thoughts from my mind. Nobody would be tossing Antonio from any cliffs.

I hoped.

The sugar high helped me crash, fast. I was tired, not having slept well. I would have called Antonio and left him a message but realized I didn't know his number. I walked back to his place, getting lost several times. I took in the scenery, astonished at the heavy graffiti on everything. Still, the ancient buildings held their old-world charm, in defiance, it seemed, of their desecration.

My foot with the blister started to hurt when the Band-Aid came loose and floated around my shoe. I hobbled to Antonio's door and heard a clatter of feet behind me.

I turned and found his overjoyed face, smiling at me.

He took me into his arms and kissed me. He dropped his key.

"See what you do to me?" he said. "I have no idea what

I'm doing when I'm with you."

"Do more, Antonio."

He grinned and grabbed my hand as soon as he'd unlocked the door. Our clothes went flying after he closed and
locked it again. We left a trail of things strewn as we kissed
one another.

"I hoped to come home and find you waiting in bed for
me," he said.

"Let me make it up to you. I'll do it right now."

He clasped his hands to my head, holding me to his face.
"Yeah, you will."

I wanted to ask about the meeting, but desire flamed from
deep within me. I'd thought about him nonstop since our
date. I wanted him so much it shocked me.

The first moment we were in his room, alone and naked,
was a sensory overload of manly cravings.

His hands roamed my body, stroking my cock. His jutted
toward me and all I could think about was having him inside me. I held his cock, afraid he'd take it from me. He
brushed my hand away and held both cocks in his hand,
holding my ass with the other. Antonio's kisses fed me, sus-
tained me as he kept up his languid cock-stroking. I felt the
pre-come leaking from us both, moistening his hand, helping his stroke pace to quicken.

He pushed me onto the bed and sucked my cock. It had
been so long since I'd had sex, I came fast. He kept his
mouth on me until I stopped quaking. He released me with a
kiss to my shaft, a sly smile on his lips. His tongue moved to
my balls, causing an erotic spasm to rush through me. He
parted my legs, pulling on my balls with his lips and tongue.
God, I was hard again.

Antonio licked my ass, glancing up at me. He must have
known the fire sparks he was striking inside me, but he kept
it up until I thought I was going to come again. He reached

56

across the bed and opened his nightstand, removing a box of rubbers. He bit into a foil square, taking out the rubber. He slid it onto his cock and poised between my open legs.

"This is all I think about," he whispered.

I grabbed his cock, kept my legs wide open and pressed him into me.

We both cried out as he entered me. His thrusts turned aggressive as I urged him on. Harder, deeper, faster, I wanted him to possess me. I felt his cock's fast eruption, even with the rubber on it. I came all over our bellies, Antonio whispering in my ear, "*Bacio.*"

I kissed him, ecstatic that he couldn't wait to be inside me too.

He pulled out, and I reached between my legs and took the condom from his cock.

"It won't taste good," he warned as I took him in my mouth, but after the initial rubbery taste, I loved sucking him. He fell back on the bed, his hand remaining on my ass as I sucked him. It was as though he just had to have contact. His cock was enormous, easily ten inches. I gave it my best shot and thought I did a great job of showing it how much I liked it. I held his balls in my hands, using only my mouth on his shaft.

"Oh God, Zeca!" he shouted, flooding my throat. I kept on him, pleased at how hard he came for me. His hand moved between my crouching thighs and grabbed my cock. When I finally released him, he smiled at me, kissing my face. He sat up, kissing a path down my body to my cock, placing a kiss on the swollen head.

"I'll say this for you, Zeca, you were right about your cock being bigger than Alex's."

"What do you mean?" I shrank away from him, jerking my cock out of his grasp. "I thought you said you didn't have sex with him."

"We didn't have sex." He reached out for me, pulling me back into his arms. He covered my body with his, staring down at me.

I wanted to run. My brother had suddenly joined us. The bed, as far as I was concerned, wasn't big enough for three.

"Zeca . . . are you jealous?"

He didn't wait for a response. He craned his head toward mine and kissed my cheeks, which felt like they were on fire.

"How sweet," he said, kissing my mouth. "Zeca, he was—we were dating. We fooled around, nothing to be jealous of."

"Are you going to do it again?"

He got up then. "Didn't we already cover this?"

He walked away from me.

"Want something to drink?" he asked over his shoulder.

His gorgeous ass made me drool. I got up and followed. He grinned as I found him in the kitchen.

He hunted in the fridge for cold water, but I wrapped myself in his arms.

"Don't get comfortable, Zeca. I want you back in that bed in a minute."

He found a bottle of Evian, uncapped it and drank half of it, and kept an arm around me. "That's better." He grimaced. "I didn't offer you some first. I'm sorry."

"I don't want water, I want you."

He dropped the bottle on the counter again, and we raced off to the bedroom. Our pace was more leisurely this time. His hand moved to my foot, circling to the back of my ankle, and I jumped.

"I knew you were in pain." He crouched down and kissed the top of my foot, like he had the other day, getting me hard again.

He put a fresh Band-Aid on my ankle, and we showered together in his surprisingly small bathroom that had no bathtub. Our cocks had minds of their own, straining toward one another.

Afterward, I dressed once again, feeling the urge to merge with him, but we were off and running. He held my hand as we crossed the road, his thumb caressing the back of my hand. We went back to the bakery, drank cappuccinos, and sat close to one another at a table on the pebbled promenade.

"I want to know about the meeting," I said.

"And I want to tell you. It went very well."

"That's good news. What did they say?"

He leaned back in his chair, but I noticed his knee still touched mine. I wondered if it was a coincidence or if, like me, he needed even that small connection.

"Well, I guess they feel I've been punished enough."

I absorbed this news. "So what does this mean? You'll get your job back here in Naples?"

He lifted his shoulders in a helpless gesture. "Your guess is as good as mine. I doubt it. I think they'll reinstate me and keep me in Capri." He laughed. "Would you like that, Zeca?"

My ecstatic grin gave me away.

"It could possibly mean a move to the other side of the island to Anacapri."

"Ooh! Capri Town's rival. We'll be like the Capulets and Montagues. Will we still be allowed to see each other?"

He smiled. "I'll make sure of it." His hand slid quickly up my thigh, and he took up his coffee cup again. "I want to keep seeing you, Zeca. I am certain of this."

"I'm feeling the same way."

"How about we do a little sightseeing, have some lunch, and then a siesta? I want to sleep with you in my arms."

I nodded eagerly. "Yes, please."

"We have a late dinner with our Swedish friends," he said. "So we have plenty of time to be alone together."

Antonio and I spent an amazing afternoon, during which he showed me all his favorite spots around Naples. Gradually I extracted more details about his work situation.

"It wasn't just a drug ring I exposed," he said as we walked along narrow cobblestone streets of tiny boutiques. "Sixty percent of all the businesses in Naples are forced to pay so-called protection money to the Camorra. One of them was my mother's restaurant."

So that's where Alex got the idea that Antonio owned a restaurant.

"I encouraged her not to pay, offering my services as protector. Naturally, the Camorra didn't like it."

This news had my head spinning. "You're lucky they didn't kill you."

"They got their revenge. They had me demoted. That, to an Italian, is sometimes worse. Humiliation is a delicious revenge dish."

"Is your mother okay?"

He got quiet then.

We stopped for lunch at a quaint little pizza place in downtown Naples. All over the city, I'd noticed pizza came in square shapes, not round. The smell was incredible, and even the street vendors had long lines of devoted customers.

"Pizza *fritta*," Antonio said. "Deep-fried pizza. It's the specialty of Napoli."

I loved when he used the Italian words for anything. I'd never tried deep-fried pizza since the tradition had never made it outside the city. It was ironic that it was deemed one of Naples' best-preserved delicacies. It hadn't even made it to Capri, which was a half-hour boat ride away. We watched the guy behind the counter make our *frittas*. Spooning a mixture of cheese, tomatoes and minced meat onto a round piece of dough, he topped it with another piece and put it in the deep fryer. The end result was about the most amazing thing I'd ever eaten in my life. Antonio and I split a small one, and I couldn't tell if the cook's expression was scandalized or amused when Antonio licked tomato coulis from the tip of my nose.

We raced on to the next wondrous sight. Antonio held my hand the whole time. I wondered when we'd have that siesta, though sleep was the furthest thing from my mind. I wanted to be naked under him as he fucked me with his relentless cock.

Antonio wanted to try on cufflinks at one boutique. I'd never seen him in formal attire until that day, and he was the only man I knew who wore them. He tried on several pair, but when I couldn't help him decide, he asked the store owner to hold the two we were torn between until the following day.

"I should have known better than to take you shopping for serious jewelry when you just want to be home in bed with me," he said.

This surprised me. "How did . . . how do you know?"

He shrugged. "I'm a good cop. I read people. Besides, I want the same thing."

We walked toward home, or at least I hoped that was where we were going.

"So cufflinks are serious jewelry?" I asked.

He laughed. "Of course. Even if I love you madly one day and wish to spend the rest of my life with you, Zeca, don't expect a wedding ring or even a wedding. I may buy you cufflinks, though."

"We were talking about your mother earlier," I reminded him.

"She's away. I sent her to a safe place, and the restaurant has been sold."

Boy, Alex got all of this stuff wrong.

Antonio paused outside a men's store selling lightweight

sweaters and rifled through the selection on a table. I was about to ask more, but he hit me with a question of his own.

"What about *your* mother?" he asked.

He might as well have punched me in the stomach. I felt the fried pizza burning in my gut. "My mother?"

"Yes, you know, the woman who gave birth to you?"

"What about her?" My voice sounded strained, even to me.

"Are you close?"

"No."

"That was quick." He left the sweaters and moved on to a pile of shirts.

"Just the truth."

"She hurt you both, didn't she?"

His tone was gentle and yet he had to know his words were like little steak knives. "No. She hurt us all."

He studied a shirt he held in his hands, but I had a feeling he was weighing his words. Waiting to pounce with a fresh thrust with his little knives. Damn. The guy had missed his true vocation. He would have made a great bullfighter.

"How much do you know?"

He dropped the shirt. "Not much. Your brother . . . well, he mentioned an accident. I thought it was a car accident, but after the way you reacted on the funicular, I suspect it was a train."

"She left my father when Alex and I were fifteen." I swallowed. Christ. It was still hard. Some days I could talk about it, some days I couldn't. In spite of this being a day I really didn't want to, I knew I would have to talk to Antonio about it.

"My mother left all three of us for some other guy she met online. It was hard for my dad. He was an actor, and people buzzed about it. We didn't hear from her for a whole year . . . until she abducted us."

He hadn't known this. I could tell by the astonished look on his face.

"She picked us up from school one day and took us to a train station. We got on the train to go meet her boyfriend out in the country, where they lived. The train jumped its track for some reason and collided with an oncoming train. We all survived, but she and I were hurt badly. There were a lot of deaths. For some reason . . . we made it."

"*Tesoro* . . . Zeca . . . I had no idea."

He took me into his arms. I could feel his heart pounding against my chest. "I would have killed her," he said against my ear.

All I could do was hug him back. He released me, and we kept walking, his fingers laced with mine.

He stopped again. "You said you were badly injured?" His fingers stroked mine.

"I broke my back. They said I'd never walk again. As you see, they were wrong."

"So this is why Alex said the accident affected you more than him."

We stopped at a light. "No. It affected him too. He just . . . I don't think he ever dealt with it. My father divorced my mother. That was some closure for all three of us."

He leaned against a lamppost, waiting for the light to change. "And how about you, Zeca? Have you dealt with it?"

"I think so. I don't speak to her. Not because of the accident but because of what she did to my father. You see, she didn't love us. Not really. I find it hard to believe a woman who loves her children would leave them in the first place."

Antonio nodded. "I couldn't imagine my mother doing that."

"She came after us to hurt Toppy. And you know what? He's a very good man. He's bat-shit crazy, but he's an actor and a man of sincere passion. He's a man who stepped up and took care of us. He stayed on that stupid TV show of his as long as he did so he could be in one place, for his family.

"People have no idea about all the jobs he turned down. Movies in America and plays on Broadway. And then my mother almost cost him his family."

Antonio gave me a long look. People crushed past us as the light changed. He took me in his arms again and held me.

"You have no idea how wonderful you are, Zeca. I'm going to take you upstairs right now and show you."

"Please do that," I said.

My spiraling emotions calmed when he got me inside. His face came down to mine, and he kissed me.

CHAPTER FIVE

We made love all afternoon, Antonio a walking dream of pleasure and physical delight. He loved making me come and seemed to enjoy the way my body responded to him. I fell asleep in his arms, sated and shaky. It felt so good when his hold tightened on me . . . until he shook me awake.

"*Bello* . . . Zeca, you're having a bad dream."

He kissed me. I was hot and sweaty, but it wasn't from having my brains fucked out.

"What happened?" I asked.

"You were doing this." He lifted his arms up and down, imitating me. I recognized the motion.

My God, I was working the stiff, ancient arms of the cappuccino machine — even in my sleep. "No wonder I wake up with sore arms every day!"

"You do?" He stared at me. "Right, I am talking to Toppy about a new coffee machine."

I laughed. "You don't have to do that."

He looked wounded.

"Only if you want to," I added.

"I want to. Your face looked . . ." He glanced away and back again. "So stressed out." I could see he was really upset.

Sitting up in bed, I confessed my recurrent nightmare of making the wrong coffees and running out of teaspoons. He didn't laugh. He looked horrified.

"My mother . . . she has the same dreams."

"I want to meet her," I said.

"You will. She will love you."

What about you? Will you love me?

I let him drag me to the shower. We had time for a quick wash before our dinner with the Swedish couple, who turned out to be amazing. Sven and Marianna were sweet and captivated by the tale of our romance. They loved being in on our secret that I was supposed to be Alex. Eager to take the attention off my still-new feelings for Antonio, I asked Sven about his work.

He willingly talked about his anthropological study. He told me about the group of children he'd interviewed, from the ages of five to seventeen. He returned twice a year to spend time with them.

"Where do they live?" I asked him.

"The Spanish Quarter in Naples."

"That's the most violent neighborhood, they say, in all of Europe," Antonio commented.

Sven was affected in particular by one little girl. I noticed the way his wife Marianna slipped her hand into his as he talked about little Lucia and her mother's life as a drug runner. I felt Antonio's hand moving into mine. I adored his touch and his constant awareness of me.

"You look much happier tonight, Antonio," Sven said. "I kept wondering why you were staring at the guy behind the counter at Café Toppy, and not the one sitting beside you."

"Now you know," Antonio said, his arm moving around me.

Sven and Marianna were also returning to Capri after the weekend, and we promised to spend more time together.

The thought of Capri clouded my joy for the moment. I had to remind myself I had three nights and two whole days with Antonio until that happened. I kept a happy smile on my face as we all shared pizza and pasta, sipping a wonderful red Taurasi wine.

After a single glass, I shared their amusement about my

brother and me switching identities. After a second glass, I laughed out loud as Antonio plotted and schemed with Sven on ways to get even with Alex.

"As long as you don't have sex with him," I said.

Antonio grinned at me. "I love how jealous you get."

Until we went home and he threw me to the ground the second we entered the apartment, I'd been worried, anxious that he might get naked again with my brother.

"I plan to punish him and teach him a lesson. Not to fuck him," Antonio said as he unbuttoned my shirt. "I am not your mother, Zeca. I'm not an asshole."

For some reason, this tickled me. I threw my legs around his waist as he lay between my thighs on the floor.

"I'm not always like this," I said, "I promise. You bring out something in me, Antonio."

"Yes. You bring it out in me, too, Zeca. You're not seeing anybody else are you?" His eyes burned into mine.

"No."

"Good. Because I will kill any man who tries to touch you."

His mouth moved to my throat and along my collarbone as I reached between our melded bodies and undid his pants. He growled as I reached through the open waistband and grabbed his cock through the top of his pants.

"Give it to me."

He grinned, sliding up my body to bring his cock to my lips. I took as much into my mouth as I could, forcing his pants down his beautiful ass and muscular thighs. He raised himself and stood before me, kicking his shoes off and removing his pants. He moved between my legs, opened my own fly and quickly licked my cock head as he freed it from my underpants. He straddled my upper body again, letting me suck his cock.

It was so big, and I wanted to enjoy all of it. I relaxed my throat, but it was hard to take him in completely in this position. I pushed him back, sitting up as he sat on my lap, letting me feast on his big dick. It was the most beautiful cock I had ever handled. I let my fingers roam to his balls and his perineum. He pulled out of my reach.

He slid my underpants and jeans all the way off my legs and told me to get on my hands and knees. Then he stuck his face right between my ass cheeks and began to lick.

I went crazy. Having my ass eaten was an incredible feeling. I pushed toward him, one hand moving back to touch his face. Oh, the man of my dreams was licking my ass! Antonio seemed to be enjoying himself back there. My cock throbbed between my legs. I couldn't stand the pressure building inside me anymore, yet I didn't want him to stop.

"Come for me," he urged, pulling my cock back toward him, milking it as he went back to sucking my ass.

I came hard, Antonio not letting up on me until I was hard and ready to erupt a second time.

He rolled me onto my back. We were too worked up to move to the bedroom, and we had no condoms on us. He rubbed his cock against my crack, his dark brown eyes melting into mine. He kissed me as he moved his cock away from my ass and held it, with mine, in his hand. He brought us both off with quick, smooth strokes, screaming out my name, collapsing on me with a multitude of kisses, my sighs silenced by his roving tongue.

Each ensuing moment of our weekend was so wonderful and filled with constant laughter and fun. He took me to dinner Saturday night at a wonderful restaurant called Umberto. We got there at nine o'clock after persuading each other that we really ought to get out of bed. Antonio knew the owners, who gave us a small table wedged between three other couples. It was perfect. He chose the wine. A Campagnian, he assured me, was one of the best of the region. We shared dishes of antipasti and fish, and his fingers kept moving under the table to grope mine.

"What would you like for dessert?" he asked me.

"I'm thinking I'm ready for some Neopolitan," I said.

"You haven't had enough of him yet?" His mouth did the quirky smile thing, and I felt my heart beating just a little faster.

"Never," I said. "I don't think I could get enough of you."

We walked arm in arm back to his place stopping for a quick coffee at the gay-friendly Caffè Intra Moenia near the apartment. A guitar player entertained us as Antonio, and I nabbed a sidewalk table. Chairs were scarce, and I was happy to give up mine and sit on his lap. We swapped kisses, our conversation flowing.

The piazza was in full bloom at midnight as we made our way home, talking about our work. Antonio asked me bluntly if I would consider continuing our relationship if he moved to Anacapri or even back to Naples. I said yes, without hesitation.

On Sunday morning I discovered that the mysterious Teresa managed a gay-friendly sauna near the Fiat dealership. You could steam in a room with others or alone. We chose to be together, and I quickly pushed my lover back against the wooden bench, sucking his cock.

He begged me to stop. He wanted to sixty-nine. Nothing doing. I wanted him to come in my mouth. I was proud when I finally managed to get all of him in my throat.

"You're going to kill me," he said when his breathing resumed its normal pace. "It's dangerous to give head like that in a sauna. I'm kinda old, you know."

"How old are you?"

"Thirty-eight."

"You *are* old," I kidded. "Ten years older than me."

Just for that, I made him come a second time.

I didn't want to return to Capri. Nothing had officially changed in Antonio's work status, and for now, he was still relegated to the challenging task of tourism. This meant he would still be on my side of the island and we both wanted to spend all our free time together. However, getting back to reality, I felt like I was about to lose my best friend.

I did better on the funicular going up than I had going down. He kept my hand in his, and I loved him for it. I think that was the moment I caved in and admitted I was a goner.

I loved this man. I let him care for me and worry about me.

Back on dry land, he held me against him for a moment. We looked up at the mountains framing the gorgeous island, and now, I was pleased to be back.

"There's something I've been meaning to ask you," Antonio said. "Did your brother even call you once this weekend?"

I shook my head.

"And you think he *likes* me?"

I grinned. "*I* do. Does that count?"

"It's the only thing that counts." He kissed me. "Zeca . . ."

"Yes?"

"Please don't tell him that I know. I have no idea how he thought he could get away with such a ridiculous scheme for an entire weekend—"

"Neither do I. I think he was counting on my feelings for you. He knows I care about you and . . . and . . . I didn't want to hurt you."

There. I'd sort of said it.

"And what feelings are those?"

I couldn't say it. It was too soon; it was ridiculous.

"Zeca. I will handle him. I will see him tonight, and I will tell him we are falling in love with each other and want to be together."

"Oh my God."

"I'm not wrong, am I?"

Christ . . . I had tears in my eyes. I'd never fallen so hard or so fast for a man. And a good man at that.

"Don't be upset." He pressed his face to mine. "I don't want to play any more games. I'm tired of games. I was so lonely and hated life until you body slammed yourself on a wave for me."

I laughed then. "Okay."

"I'll talk to him and get his blessing. That means I won't see you tonight. I'll ask him out instead."

"Do you have to?"

"Yes, I have to." He smiled. "No more secrets and lies. I want to be with *you*. I want to spend time with Zeca. But I need a few words with Alex first."

We said goodbye, and I realized I still didn't know where he lived on Capri. At least I had his phone number now, and he had mine. I checked my watch. Still early. It was eight a.m. A strange lull time between coffee addicts and hungry tourists. I walked to the café and found it empty of customers and my father reinstalling the old coffee grinder behind the counter. He jumped back, a guilty look on his face.

"What are you doing?" I was astounded.

"Don't sneak up on a person," he griped.

"Where did you find it? I thought I chucked it out."

"You did. I took it out again."

"Oh, Dad."

"How was your weekend?"

"Spectacular."

"Geez, mate. I need some bloody sunglasses. Your afterglow is blinding me."

I grinned at him.

Dad started fiddling with the coffee grinder again. "I'm only half kidding. I'm so glad to see you happy."

"Thanks, Dad. How was your weekend?"

"Don't ask."

"Why? What happened?"

He gave an exaggerated sigh. "You want coffee?"

"Sure."

I felt a strange quivering sensation in my body. I was on planet pheromones. I turned and saw Antonio walking toward me. My body didn't stop reacting. The man did things to my insides that nobody had ever done to me before. His intent gaze was on me.

"You want a coffee?" my dad asked.

"I'd love that, Toppy, thank you." He leaned closer to me, and I thought the heat could have warmed a hundred cities. My father wrestled with the coffeemaker and as soon as he was distracted and the noise deafening, Antonio leaned even closer.

"*Bacio*," he said.

I couldn't have kept my mouth off him if I tried. My cell phone rang. I checked the readout. Alex.

"Hey," Alex said. "How was your weekend?"

"Good. How was yours?"

Antonio was gesturing to me frantically. He grabbed the order pad on the counter and scribbled a note. "Don't tell him I'm with you."

"Mine was okay. Hugh's gone. I dunno . . . I want to talk to you about it. That friggin' Mrs. Pampina turned up in Portofino."

"She did?"

"It was bizarre. I don't think she realizes I'm gay. I spent my whole weekend hiding behind potted palms and holding my breath underwater."

"Just tell her you're gay," I suggested.

Antonio's eyes widened. He stared at me as my conversation continued.

"Well . . . I'm not so sure about that, Zec. I'm dreaming about titties now. I'm thinking maybe I'm bisexual."

Bisexual? *Alex?*

"I'm confused, Zeec. It caused some problems this weekend with Hugh."

"You like him, don't you?"

"I don't know. We argued the whole time. I found myself . . . I dunno, thinking about her."

"Is that why you argued?"

"That, and also I'm confused about Antonio."

My heart sank. If things hadn't worked out with Hugh, he'd set his sights on Antonio once again.

Dad slid the coffees over to us, and Antonio took them to the table.

"Anyway, I'm coming back from Portofino. I'm on the ferry. I should be there in about half an hour. You pulled it off, didn't you?"

I had visions of Antonio's lovely cock in my hands and mouth. "Yeah. I pulled it off."

"Cool. Hey, thanks for covering for me. I hope you didn't wear him out too much."

I didn't say anything. I saw the distaste flicker across my lover's face. Clearly, he could hear every word.

"You still with him?"

"No."

"Any idea where he is?" Alex asked.

"No."

"You'll have to fill me on all the details before I see him. You had a good time together? He was nice to you?"

"Very good. And yes . . . he was wonderful to me."

I ended the call, and Antonio's mouth nuzzled my free ear.

"I want a clean start for us, Zeca. I don't want Alex to have any illusions about a relationship with me, but I want to handle this my way. Okay?"

"Okay."

Antonio's cell rang.

"Cool. I'll see you later."

My lover took the call and left the café, murmuring into his phone, leaving his coffee untouched.

"May as well drink it," Dad said, and flopped into the seat beside me.

I saw Antonio pacing outside.

"What's the plan?" Dad asked, and I told him.

"Oh boy. Your brother isn't going to willingly hand him over, you know."

"You don't think?" I was suddenly very depressed.

"Do you know Alex at all, kid?"

I closed my eyes. I had a horrible feeling I'd have to choose between my brother and my new lover. I didn't want to be without either one of them.

"Antonio seems like a nice guy; maybe he can persuade your brother. Maybe it won't even be a problem," Dad said.

"He says he's now sexually confused. Mrs. Pampina's stampeding after him."

"She's an attractive woman," Dad said, stirring his coffee. "She's missing some hardware though. I think Alex likes dicks."

I took a mouthful of coffee and almost sprayed it across the room.

The thought that Antonio wanted a future with me cheered me up. He was so old-school and gentlemanly. He wanted things squared away between him and Zeca. I liked that. Antonio not only got loads of charm when he came out of the birth canal but character too. I turned my focus to semi-geriatric love and asked my dad about his weekend with Angelina.

"She's schizo," he announced. "Crazy as a fruit bat."

He went on to tell me how she played games with him all weekend and to top it off, didn't even bake her famous cinnamon bread on Sunday. All I could think was that my brother would be seeing the man I loved that night.

And I wouldn't.

We were slammed all day at the café, and when it was time for siesta, Dad stomped home, grumpy after a heated conversation on the phone with Angelina. I felt restless and nervous. I didn't want to go home. I wanted to be with Antonio. I hadn't seen my brother since his return and hadn't heard from Antonio again. I walked away from the town center and across the piazza, toward the cliffs. I'd promised myself and God I would pay my respects to the Virgin Mary if I survived the funicular. I bought some red roses at the florist and found my way to the Virgin's grotto, surprised to see the statue was on a ledge behind glass and many people had left offerings around her stone enclosure.

I placed my roses through the iron bars around the ledge and looked around me. We were quite high up, about thirty feet from the ground. I was alone with her. I felt ridiculous at first, but once I started talking, I couldn't stop.

"I'm sorry I haven't been before, and I'm sorry that the first time I come to visit you, I'm asking you for help."

It was weird. I realized I heard no sounds. No people, no birds . . . nothing. It was as if she'd stopped the music so she could listen to me.

"I need your help. I love this man . . . or at least I think I do. No. I know I do. I keep thinking about what my dad said to me the other day. You have to love before you can be relentless. I think I know what he means now and I know I've never felt this way before. I think I could love this man forever. I could love Antonio with the relentless passion he deserves."

I started to cry. Boy, I was a big, blubbering dope. For years, I'd pent up all my feelings and it fucking hurt. *Oops. I thought of a swear word. In front of the Celestial Virgin!*

For a moment I let the tears fall. I gathered my thoughts.

Love is not a train wreck. Love does not have to end in grief and seven months in the hospital.

I spoke to the Virgin again.

"If you help me, if you just give me the chance to see if this works"—I touched the roses through the iron bars—"there's more where these came from."

I heard the sound of voices. Somebody was climbing up the side of the mountain. I whispered "goodbye" to the Virgin and walked back toward town, feeling hopeful. I went home, realizing I'd left my overnight bag at the café. I didn't care. I'd wash my clothes later. I had little time for a nap, but I decided I'd be grumpy with just a short one. I showered and changed to feel a little fresher for the evening shift. It hurt that I hadn't heard a single word from Antonio.

A little voice inside me said, *Trust him.*

The evening shift at the café was gruesome. Dad was in a foul mood, and my brother was AWOL. Things between my father and Angelina must have been bad because we didn't receive our second order of baked goods for the day. I had to leave the café and deal with it since Toppy was afraid she would throw the bread at him rather than give it to him.

Angelina was barely civil, but she had no real bone to pick with me. She kept telling me my father was *pazzesco*, crazy, but was too busy to explain why as she stuffed a large wicker basket full of loaves. I began to understand she wanted my father's attention, but from what he told me, she kept pushing him away.

"He loves you," I said, interrupting her Italian tirade.

"Why does he think I am going to leave him if I even go to the bathroom?" she asked.

"Because my mother went to the shop to buy milk one day and never came home."

Her mouth dropped into a big, expressive O. A guilt-stricken look crossed her face. Maybe I shouldn't have said anything, but it seemed to me that I needed to learn a little more about being relentless in love, and so did Angelina.

I arrived back at the café and was stunned to see Antonio and my brother strolling out of it, arm in arm.

"Hey," Alex said.

I was surprised I was still standing. The agony of seeing him in Antonio's company was excruciating. I glanced at Antonio, whose gaze was on my brother's face.

"I haven't seen you since we got back from Naples," Alex said. He winked.

What an ass.

"How was Naples?" I asked. I couldn't believe my brother thought he could get away with this. We hadn't even talked about the weekend and what Antonio and I had done. How was he going to bluff his way through their evening?

Then I remembered Antonio's plan to expose Alex. He didn't look like he was in an expository mood. More like he was in an exploratory one. He was all over Alex, who was also all over him. What the fuck? Had I taken the wrong kind of flowers to the Celestial Virgin? Had my entire weekend with this man been fake?

Alex rubbed up against Antonio, who responded.

It was sickening. I couldn't watch. I turned and walked into the café, and my dad stared at me.

"Your boyfriend sure looks happy to see your brother."

"Yeah, doesn't he?"

"And I thought women were confusing." He snatched the basket from me and stomped off to the kitchen.

We Colombo men were big on stomping. How was it that Dad and I were having such a bad night and my wayward brother was basking in Antonio's presence?

I'd never been so glad to finish a shift as I was that night. I closed up with Dad, and we sipped a couple of restorative limoncellos together. We ignored the tourists bashing hopefully at the windowpanes.

"Go away, ugly people," my dad said under his breath. We thought we were the funniest, suavest guys alive. Limoncello will do that to a fellow.

And then he got a call from Angelina. He ran off like a happy, horny teenager to meet her at her house.

Checking that my cell phone worked, I turned off all the lights, sat behind the counter and listened to Cecilia Bartoli as I watched the passersby. I drank a third limoncello. It definitely put me in a less funky mood as I locked up and headed home.

I was halfway up the stairs when my brother called, screaming at me.

"Don't think for one fucking moment that I will agree to this relationship! You embarrassed me, Zeec! How the fuck could you dare? He fucking knew it was you and you fucked him? And now you want to be with him?"

"Please, Alex. I love him."

"Fuck you," he screamed again and hung up on me.

I lay on my bed trying to remain calm. He came home half an hour later and walked straight to my room. He was in the mood for vengeance, and it shocked me how angry he was.

"He's *my* lover. I found him first," Alex fumed as he flipped on my bedroom lights.

I sat up on my bed, ready for battle. "He says you weren't

lovers."

"We did everything but." He spat the words out at me.

"You left him. You dumped him for another man. We discovered we really care for each other."

"It's bullshit, and you know it. He prefers *me*. You pretended to be me all weekend. That's who he wants."

"No. He knew before then."

That surprised him, I could tell. Alex seemed to sag a little.

"I couldn't believe it," he said, sitting on my bed. "One moment he's kissing me, the next he's telling me I'm an asshole and that he's in love with *you*."

"He said that? That he's in love with me?"

"Oh, shut up, Zeca! It's not over between him and me. We agreed to speak again tomorrow. He now says he's confused and will not call you until he gives me a second chance." He leaned toward me. "He will not call you *or* take your calls. So don't even think about it."

It was as if he'd slugged me right on the chin. I went numb. I sat there long after he had gone and stared into space. Antonio was confused?

I had a rotten night's sleep, wondering how much of what Alex had told me was true. I didn't believe half of what he said, and yet the evidence was there. Antonio's silence.

I got up early, showered, changed and went to work. I went through the motions. The coffee grinder fritzed on me, and I smashed it in the back room. I juggled sixteen coffee drinkers on my own, and the unthinkable happened—I made all the wrong coffees. I almost laughed out loud. My nightmare had come true, really complete with the realization I also had no clean teaspoons either.

By the time I broke for siesta, there was still no word from Antonio. I thought I would die from the grief I felt.

My father woke me at six. I'd slept three hours and felt like shit.

"I told you he'd be a little bastard. Come on, let's go the café."

"Why did I survive the train wreck, Dad? Why?"

My father became hysterical. "Don't you ever say that. Never! I need you, Zeca!"

I sat on my bed, willing myself not to cry. I wanted to be relentless. I wanted to be loving and loved.

He put his arms around me.

"Have faith," he said, and I wondered if he'd ever been to visit the Celestial Virgin.

We walked down to the café. My crazy dad was my rock. He kept up a soothing mantra of, "You'll be okay, you'll see."

Down by the piazza I could hear violins playing. Somebody was getting married. I remembered how Antonio said he would never marry me. He would give me cufflinks. Serious jewelry. We'd never gone back to the shop to pick out the pair of cufflinks he would buy. We'd been too busy making love.

Tons of people were waiting for us to open, including Sven and Marianna. They were sweet and patient as Dad, and I dealt with all the hungry mouths to feed. Alex was missing and not responding to calls.

Antonio shocked me by turning up midway through the evening. I knew he was there because I felt him. It was like heaven and hell; as if I was a junkie who'd caught sight of the needle, but wasn't close enough to plunge it into my veins. I stopped wielding the coffee machine's arm mechanism, and it whooshed out steam right into my face.

He was miserable, I could see that. He hovered in the doorway, caught sight of our friends waiting at their table and after a long look around the restaurant, came right over to me.

"We need to talk. It won't take long."

"Go," Dad said. "In the kitchen. I'll hold things steady."

As soon as we'd crossed the kitchen and hit the storeroom, he was all over me. Our hands and mouths roamed one another. His kisses were gorgeous, balm to my toxic shock.

"You haven't called me," he teased when we finally paused for breath.

"Neither have you. Alex said you were confused."

Antonio snorted. "I agreed I wouldn't call you until he and I talked again. It doesn't surprise me that he would lie and try to hurt you. You didn't believe him, did you?"

He could tell by my face that I had.

"I didn't want to believe him."

"Your brother is a flake. I have no idea what's going on with him, but he's playing games. He doesn't want me but becomes hysterical at the idea of you and me being together. He said he wanted to talk tonight and I gave him a chance. He just blew it. He never showed up. I was never confused about my feelings for Alex. I'm confused by his behavior."

"But you didn't call." I tried not to pout. It was unmanly to begin with and futile when he was kissing me nonstop.

"No, I didn't call because I'm a man of my word. I did *not* promise I wouldn't come here for a bite of supper with my very dear friends Sven and Marianna."

I grinned at him, reaching up for another kiss.

Antonio's expression became guarded. "I'm going to settle this thing with him once and for all. If he doesn't agree to us being together, what then?"

"I can't give you up," I said. "I just can't."

A knock at the door roused us from our hot exchange. I noticed the bulge in Antonio's pants, and I was once again uncomfortable too, but it sure beat the heck out of being miserable.

A couple of times over their meal, I caught his smile and Sven's. Marianna hugged me goodbye, and my dad flirted harmlessly with her. It killed me to give Antonio a friendly wave.

And then I saw my brother running across our front doors to him.

They walked off together, and I tried not to let my spirits sink. Dad and I drank several limoncello together that night and walked . . . well, *staggered* home very late.

It was around three in the morning when I heard someone calling my name.

"Zeca!" A pebble hit my window. I looked down and was amazed to see it was Antonio. He was a welcome sight to be sure but what the hell was he doing here before dawn? I was so heart-stung by seeing his beautiful face it took me a few seconds to absorb that Sven was there too.

"Your brother still says no, but I need you. Sven helped me carry this ladder all the way up those stairs. The Capulets and the Montagues . . . we must never be apart. I'm a creative man, you know."

"So I see." I stared at the ladder leaning against the wall outside my window. "Get up here." I thrust my arms down to him, and my lover scrambled up the rungs. I pulled him through the window, and we looked down, waving at Sven before he lumbered away, the ladder under his arm.

"He's so nice," I said. "He really likes you."

"He likes *us*. I told him we'd go to Sweden to visit them for Christmas."

"Christmas?"

"I adore Swedish cookies."

Antonio made me laugh, but his expression was fierce as he pulled off my boxer briefs, moaning when my cock sprang out at him.

"Look at this delicious treat," he crooned, his tongue swirling over my cock head. "Oh, this is so much tastier than cookies, Zeca."

We pawed and tongued each other and then he was between my open thighs. I kept up a mantra of *fuck me, fuck me* until finally he reached into his pocket and pulled out a rubber. He pulled his pants down.

"I'm always ready for you now." He grinned as he sheathed his cock and let me have it. I let him close off my impassioned noises with his savage kisses as we came together, my arms above my head, pinned to the pillow.

"You are one hot fuck," he whispered into my mouth.

"So are you." I pushed him off me and onto his back against the bed. I ripped off the rubber.

"I can't wait until I can be inside you without one of those," he said.

"That means more to me than cufflinks."

He laughed. "I am glad you think so."

Antonio came to work with me the next morning. We sneaked by my father's room. His door was open, the room empty. He must have gotten lucky with his mercurial neighbor. But my brother's room was *not* empty. I saw a tangle of long, dark curls.

Mrs. Pampina!

Antonio and I stood staring at my brother, who snuggled into our neighbor. Their steady breathing assured us we hadn't woken them.

I closed the door as we tiptoed away.

We walked down to the village together. "What the fuck?" Antonio mused. "Is he straight now?"

"He told me he's confused."

"Confused? I would say. Wonder if Hugh knows."

"Do you care?" I asked.

"Of course not."

"What happened when you talked to Alex?"

He shrugged and took my hand as we negotiated the stairs. "We argued. He talked a lot of nonsense. He just can't stand being rejected. I don't want to have that discussion again."

I nodded. I felt anxious about going against my brother's wishes, but his behavior sure was bizarre.

Halfway down the steps, Antonio stopped me. "There's something you should know."

"What?"

He hesitated.

"Come on, out with it."

"The first time I asked him out, I thought he was you. He pretended he *was* you and only admitted the truth later. By then, I liked him."

I couldn't believe what I was hearing. "He pretended he was me and you still wanted to go out with him?"

"Zeca, are you mad? You're wonderful. Don't you see that? Do I need to tell you?"

"Yes, Antonio, you do."

He showed me instead. In the men's restroom of the café, we had a stone-cold quickie with the front doors wide open and our hearts pounding. He had me up against the wall of the narrow stall, my legs around his waist. He had trouble getting the rubber on, but he must have had practice. Relief was swift. I came in his hand as he erupted deep inside me, telling me he loved me

"*Il mio bello uomo*, my beautiful man," he said in my ear.

We cleaned up, and he helped me with the morning shift. He laughed as I taught him how to make the coffee. Actually, he was more of a distraction than actual help, and he made me promise I would teach him to make perfect foam. We sipped our first coffees of the morning, and I fondled his ass as we stood behind the counter.

"What time do you take your break?" he asked.

"Three o'clock."

He nodded. "I'll pick you up, Montague. I have something special planned."

I hated seeing him go, but we'd had yet another magical evening together. I kept smiling, thinking about Sven helping him with the ladder.

My siesta break came fast. I'd been so busy the time just flew. Antonio arrived, grabbed my hand and my dad rolled his eyes.

"I'll lock up, shall I?"

"Have you been to the Blue Grotto?" Antonio asked me. I hadn't. I was stoked to find that he'd booked a private boat with a very old oarsman, who rowed us through the small hole in the cliff face at the bottom of the island by the marina. People swirled around us on bigger boats as part of tours. But I was the lucky one. I had Antonio all to myself. I was torn between gazing at him and drinking in the incredible beauty around me. We sat together, Antonio's arm around me as we glided through the dark caves. Fairy lights hidden in crevices twinkled; the water shimmered in its turquoise beauty.

We'd just entered paradise.

The old man began to sing "Caro Mio Ben."

"It's my favorite song," I whispered to Antonio. "How did you know?"

He shrugged. "You keep singing it to me." He touched his heart. "In here."

The old man didn't stop singing as Antonio held me to him, kissing me.

Chapter Six

We planned to meet that night for supper when I finished work. My dad invited Antonio in for a limoncello, and he ranted about how Alex had been shirking his responsibilities all week.

"My car is still at the bloody mechanic in Naples. Do you know how much the shipping cost me?"

"I can find a buyer for you," Antonio said. "For a lot more than you paid for it."

"Really?" All the rage seemed to evaporate from my father. He was one of those guys who abhorred a bad investment. Unfortunately, he was the kind who frequently made one too.

I glanced at my cherished and adored Mr. Fixit. Antonio smiled back at me. I hoped I was about to get a kiss when Dad was verbally off and running again.

"That Angelina. I swear. She gets weirder and weirder."

"What now?" I asked.

"She gets mad at me all the time. Can you believe it? Me! I'm a sweetheart, I am."

"You're crazy," I said.

"What's that got to do with anything?" he asked. "You're as mad as a hatter, but you're still a sweet guy."

"Me? What's this got to do with me?"

"He's right, *bello*. You are beautiful, crazy . . . and I am in love with you," Antonio said, looking a little moon-faced.

And then a bizarre thing happened.

Mrs. Pampina came in, her eyes red-rimmed.

86

"Have you heard?" she asked. She was wearing a fire-engine-red sundress, the hundredth provocative dress I'd seen her wear recently. It was so tight I could see her belly-button underneath the fabric around her waist. She pressed a tissue to her nose.

"Heard what?" my dad asked.

"Your son!" She pointed at my father, then over her shoulder. "He's with *your* girlfriend. I saw them in your house."

"With *my* Angelina?"

"He stood me up. We had a date. He says he's in love with her!"

She ran out as fast as her tight skirt would allow, leaving the three of us sitting there.

"Did I just hear her say she had a date with . . . Alex?" Dad asked.

"No, of course not," I said.

"She said so," Antonio said.

"But he isn't straight, he's — "

"An idiot," Antonio said.

"He ran off with my girlfriend? I'll kill him." Dad thumped the table. "And he keeps hiding from me to keep from having to pay for my bloody car. Killing my car is one thing, stealing my woman . . . this time, he's gone too far!"

Dad ran from the restaurant, leaving Antonio and me to lock up. I wasn't quite sure what to make of the news. I glanced at Antonio, who was watching me.

"What?" I asked, trying to read his expression.

He shrugged. "It lets us off the hook. We can be together now."

I sighed. "We would be together anyway."

"Good, because I've accepted an assignment right here in Capri Town and I'd sure hate to have to avoid you for the rest of my life."

"I'd hate that, too, Capulet."

He leaned in and kissed me.

"So, I suppose we should go up to the house and mediate."

I grinned. "Well, you *are* the tourist police."

"Does he fall for women often?" Antonio asked.

"No. He's always had a thing for older women, but never, as far as I know, sexually. Until last night. I think he still misses our mother."

"Do you?"

"No."

"That's okay, I'll share mine with you."

"I'd like that." I rinsed out our limoncello glasses. "Can I ask you a question?"

"Fire away."

I paused, wondering how to phrase it. "You seem very . . . blasé about the fact that your father had a mistress."

"Really?" He shook his head. "It's not how I felt. I was hurt. I was surprised. It was . . . kind of my train wreck."

"I'll never betray you, Antonio. I'm sorry he hurt you."

"Thank you."

"My father and I, we're dreamers. He taught me a wonderful expression. He taught me that I have to be relentless about love . . . about my love for you."

"Love is like that," he said. "Which is why I'm here and so are you."

"I'm worried about my father. I wasn't kidding when I said he's nuts."

"He'll be fine. We'll go check on him, okay?" He looked at our store shelves. "Maybe we should take him some limoncello. And for us too. I'd like to pour some on your cock and balls and lick it off in bed tonight."

I reached for a bottle. "You know, I still have no idea where you live."

"I'll show you, right after we check on Toppy."

He helped me check all the doors one last time then we headed up to the house, hand in hand. Antonio pulled me to him, hugging me.

"Don't worry. Trust me. I'm the tourist cop around here."

"There's a big difference between losing beach balls and absconding lovers," I said.

"*Bello,* you'd be surprised how attached some foreigners get to their beach balls."

I laughed. "I still can't get over Alex doing this. Or Angelina."

"I've known Angelina longer than Toppy has. She's an old family friend. She did this to get his attention. Your brother, on the other hand, maybe he's really straight. This is a possibility he presented to me the other night."

"Really?"

"Yes, really. I think we'll need to find him a nice, mature, available woman. One who can keep him in check."

"You know someone like that?"

"I know a few people. I adore playing matchmaker, you know."

"I adore *you,* Antonio."

Up at the house, when we finally got there, Mrs. Pampina was sobbing.

"He's *fa-gaysie?*" she kept screaming. It was the Italian word for gay. "He left me for a . . . man?"

"Alex likes dick," Dad said, snuggling up to Angelina.

Mrs. Pampina's mouth fell open.

"Don't panic, breathe," Antonio said, his hand rubbing comforting circles between her shoulder blades. She looked at him, her face turning red.

"Breathe," he said again. And she did.

She ran from the house, still wailing, her tight dress finally giving up its fight and splitting all the way up her back.

She shrieked, clutching the folds of fabric across her ass.

"Imagine, thinking my Angelina came here looking for Alex." Dad nuzzled his trophy baker.

Angelina giggled. "I came to bring you bread," she said, as my father buried his face in her voluptuous breasts. They stood and drifted out the back door.

Antonio held me. "This is too Italian, even for me."

"We have the house to ourselves," I said, "not to mention this swell bottle of limoncello."

"But, Montague, I want to be alone with you. Let's go to my house."

"I'd love that."

He gave me a damn good, heart-stopping kiss. I snatched up a couple of loaves of Angelina's bread from the huge basket sitting on our coffee table.

"Bring more, Zeca. Your feet won't be touching the ground anytime soon once I get you in bed," Antonio warned. We walked out the front door and immediately heard a strange grunting. We followed the sound.

I wished we hadn't.

Mr. Pampina was flat on his back, his mad wife atop him right in their front yard. She was riding him like a demented bronco.

Antonio and I averted our gazes, trying not to laugh as we took the stairs down to the piazza. I could smell the warm bread, the scent of lemon and love on the air.

"I would love to show my passion for you in public like that," he said. "I think I am jealous, Zeca. You and I might be arrested, but for them . . ." He shrugged. "It's okay."

It was the first time I'd ever seen him downcast. "You can fuck me in public any time you like, Antonio."

His face lit up. I held his hand to my lips and kissed it, borrowing one of his moves. His gaze smoldered in the semi-darkness.

"Where do you live?" I asked, juggling loaves from one hand to the other. "How far? How long must I wait to have you?"

"Not far, sexy man."

We walked in the opposite direction of the café, toward the Virgin's grotto. He pointed out a cute little cottage nestled on a slope right near her. I should have guessed he was near my favorite holy spirit.

He reached for my hand again, drawing me closer to him.

From across the piazza, a tall, sobbing figure approached us. It was my brother's boyfriend, Hugh.

"You're drenched," I said. "What happened?"

"I jumped off the cruise ship. I almost got eaten by a shark." He looked spooked. When he turned at the sound of running feet, I saw his torn shirt and traces of blood.

My brother ran toward him. "You stupid bastard!" he shouted, throwing himself into Hugh's arms.

Antonio grinned at me. "Love," he said, "has a way of fixing things itself."

"No." I shook my head. "It's because of you. You turn up, and things go right."

Under the dark Capri moon, with people still walking the piazza, he held me in his arms.

"I love you," I told him.

"I love you, too."

"*Bacio,*" he said.

And I did.

ZECA'S CAPRI LIMONCELLO

Ingredients
  10 lemons
  1 (750-ml) bottle of vodka
  3 ½ cups water
  2 ½ cups sugar

Directions

Using a vegetable peeler, remove the peel from the lemons in long strips (reserve the lemons for another use). With a small, sharp knife, trim away the white pith from the lemon peels; discard the pith. Put the lemon peels in a 2-quart pitcher. Pour the vodka over the peels and cover with plastic wrap. Steep the lemon peels in the vodka for 4 days at room temperature.

Stir the water and sugar in a large saucepan over medium heat until the sugar dissolves, about 5 minutes. Cool completely. Pour the sugar syrup over the vodka mixture. Cover and let stand at room temperature overnight. Strain the limoncello through a mesh strainer. Discard the peels. Transfer the limoncello to bottles. Seal the bottles and refrigerate until cold, at least four hours. Keeps up to one month.

You may also enjoy the following from eXtasy Books Inc:

Relentless Love
A.J. Llewellyn

Excerpt

"Hi, Alex," Antonio said.

I put a hand on his shoulder as he blew past me. "How do you do that?"

Antonio stopped. "Do what?"

"How can you tell us apart? You always do that, even when Zeca and I dress alike."

He gave me a disarming smile. "You really want to know?"

"Yeah. I really want to know."

He leaned in, and I got a whiff of peppermint gum. He put his lips to my ear. "When I see your brother, my cock gets hard, and my heart beats faster."

"Shit."

He shrugged. "You asked."

I felt a weird gravitational pull and realized Zeca was in the room. He and Antonio stood, staring at one another. The sudden whoosh of heat between them was like opening an oven door. Without a word, they walked to the kitchen together.

"Has it been busy?" Toppy asked, his toothsome movie star grin on display. Dad loved the attention he got. He happily posed for photos with his fans, autographed their menus and travel guides, even their leftover boarding passes from their plane travel. I wondered how quickly these items would wind up on eBay.

Toppy Colombo was still a handsome man, with crinkly blue eyes and dark hair helped a little—well, a lot—by hair dye. He looked amazing for a guy in his fifties. Zeca and I had just turned twenty-six and had his more dominant genes. I glanced through the service window, noting Antonio and Zeca were nowhere to be seen. Man, their dicks would drop off at the rate they were doing it.

I scooped up empty dishes and coffee cups.

"Bring me a cafe latté, Zeca . . . I mean Alex," Toppy said airily, waving his hand at me.

Bastard. He knows I can't work the damn machine. I was about to go and rain on my brother's romantic parade when he and Antonio clattered out of the stockroom, their faces shining. Antonio tucking his shirt into his pants, my brother buttoning up his Levi's fly. Oh brother.

"Dad wants a cappuccino," I said.

"You want one, too?" he asked Antonio, his fingers trailing across his lover's lips.

Antonio kissed them. "Yes," he said. "I live for your coffees."

Oh man . . . could he be any cornier?

They drifted into the restaurant as I dumped the dirty dishes in the kitchen sink. I saw Antonio taking a seat at a table for two. I noticed the possessive way he watched my brother working, oblivious to the looks on the faces of half the women in the restaurant. Antonio attracted a lot of attention. He was a big, macho guy. You'd never guess he was gay, except I knew he had big, macho feelings for my brother.

"You got any gay brothers or cousins?" I asked him, taking a seat beside him.

Antonio looked a bit startled. "Me?" He frowned. "I know a few guys . . . but none of your games would work on them, Alex."

"Games?" Shit.

He'd already lost interest in the conversation. He was back to staring at Zeca again.

One of the British women from the next table came over with a Capri street map. She batted her eyelids at Antonio and stuck her chest out at him.

I confess, I love men, but something about a big bosom enthralls me. I can't explain it. My father once said I enjoyed breastfeeding hugely when I was a baby. Our mother had abandoned us when Zeca and I were teenagers. Maybe I had a mother complex or something.

"Excuse me, officer," the woman said. "My friend and I," she pointed to a woman sitting at the table whose boobs were bursting out of her off-the-shoulder blouse, "we're visiting Capri, and we were wondering if you know where the Villa Potania is . . . we seem to have lost our way."

"Villa Potania?" Antonio took hold of the street map and pointed to a small side street off the Capri Town square. "It's just two blocks from here."

"Can you show us the way?"

"Yes. I'm showing you right here." His finger traced the line on the map.

Zeca arrived with cappuccinos for Dad, Antonio and even for me. That touched me. I had to admit, Zeca had a magical way with coffee.

"Sit awhile," he said to me. "You've been busy all morning."

Antonio gazed at my brother's crotch, then up at his face. "Vi ringrazio, bell'uomo."

My brother smiled back. I sighed inwardly. Thank you, beautiful man. It was a lovely thing to say, and the emotion behind it almost unglued me. I brushed all thoughts of Hugh from my mind. Zeca seemed to find it hard to tear himself away as he went to greet two new arrivals. The woman with the street map stood beside us, looking uncertain for a moment.

"Can you show us the way?" she asked Antonio again.

A look of confusion crossed his face. "The way to where?"

Man, my brother must have blown the guy's brains out in the stockroom.

"I'll take you." Dad's voice boomed over their conversation. The woman looked dismayed but had no choice. She waited for Dad to finish his coffee. He was such a flirt. He kept up a running patter of jokes about the island, but the woman beside us kept staring at Antonio, who was busy flicking through cell phone messages.

"Gotta get back to work," he said. "The pickpockets have been busy this morning." He caught my brother's eye and winked at him before leaving, walking down the street with his coffee cup in hand. Only in Capri.

I wanted to chase after him. I wanted to promise I wouldn't play games with his friends, but I had the second-best thing to getting Antonio to work on my behalf. I had his other half. My brother . . . who was also my other half.

Cornering him in the kitchen, I put the idea to Zeca. I wanted my own macho Italian guy.

"Are you serious?" he asked as he sliced up some of Angie's freshly baked lemon and honey bread that he would use to make French toast. "No games?"

"What is it with you and Antonio?" Before he could respond, I assured him, "No games. Please, Zeca. I want to be in love. I want a great guy."

He looked up from his perfect slices and must have taken me at my word.

"All right," he said. "I'm on it."

I took a deep breath. I felt a huge weight lifting from my shoulders and from the pit of my stomach. I wanted a guy by Valentine's Day, but I could handle it being a bit later than that. I'd just spend the day in bed with the covers over my head until it was over.

I realized nobody was waiting on tables since Toppy was still attempting to charm the two female tourists, and I ran into the restaurant—just in time to see a guy crouched behind the counter, trying to break into the cash register.

ABOUT THE AUTHOR

A.J. Llewellyn is the author of almost three hundred published gay romance novels. A.J. lives in California, but dreams of living in Hawaii. Frequent trips to all the islands, bags of Kona coffee in the fridge and a healthy collection of Hawaiian records keep A.J. refueled.

A.J's passion for the islands led to writing a play about the last ruling monarch of Hawaii, Queen Lili'uokalani. A.J. has written a non-erotic novel about the overthrow of her kingdom written in diary form from her maid's point of view.

A.J. never lacks inspiration for male/male erotic romances and has to prise fingers from the computer keyboard to pursue other passions: collecting books on Hawaiiana, surfing and spending time with family, friends and animal companions.

A.J. Llewellyn believes that love is a song best sung out loud.

Webpage: www.ajllewellyn.com
Facebook: www.facebook.com/aj.llewellyn
Twitter: www.twitter.com/ajllewellyn
Email: ajllewellyn@gmail.com

OTHER TITLES BY A.J LLEWELLYN

Available at eXtasy Books
   Temptation Eyes
   Night School Vampire
   The Fetish Café
   The Crimson Cat
   Island Heat

   Fawnskin
   Fawnskin
   Frenzied

   The House Of Driscoll
   The House of Driscoll
   Precious Blood

   BLACK POINT
   Black Point
   Back to Black Point
   Black Point Revisited
   Black Point Surrendered
   Black Point Christmas
   Black Point Forever

   Blood Eclipse
   Blood Eclipse
   Rapture
   City of Blood
   Apocalypse